The Dog Prince

The Dog Prince

Sharon Henegar

Saturday Books

Published by Saturday Books
PO Box 4592
Salem, OR 97302

ISBN: 978-0-9840648-0-9 (Trade paperback)
Henegar, Sharon L.
The dog prince / Sharon L. Henegar
McGuire, Louisa (Fictitious Character)—Fiction
Antique Dealers—Fiction
Dogs—Fiction
Humorous Fiction
Mystery Fiction

Book 3: Willow Falls series

Dedicated to Marcia Tungate,
who knows I couldn't have written this without her.

And always, for Steven.

The Dog Prince

1

The May sunshine was already hot as it sparkled on the collection of frogs strewn across a rickety card table. I was running late and had forty miles to drive. The battery on my cell phone had died, so I couldn't call and say I'd be late. I stopped to look at the frogs anyway.

And put into motion a chain of events that included mayhem and murder. I tell you, you just never know what will turn up at a good flea market.

As I picked up the frog that caught my eye, a man's voice in a plummy English accent intoned from behind me, "What a beautiful bird the frog are!" I looked over my shoulder. The man who had spoken looked to be in his mid to late thirties, with fashionably tousled hair and amazingly white teeth. He must eat bleach for breakfast.

"I beg your pardon?"

1

"It's from an old nursery rhyme," he explained. "'What a beautiful bird the frog are, When he sit he stand almost'—"

I laughed. "But I know that one! Except the version I learned was 'wonderful bird' instead of beautiful. I loved the line about 'when he hop he fly almost' and how 'when he sits he sits on what he ain't got almost.'"

"You know, I do believe you're right," he nodded. "Wonderful indeed." He smiled, but his eyes constricted to cold slits that didn't go with the smile.

A host of characters reside in my head, and one or another of them is always ready to venture an opinion. This time it was the catty one. "Look out, he's probably one of those men who can't stand to be corrected. Like Roger."

The mere thought of my dead husband was enough to make me babble. "When I got my dog, Emily Ann, she reminded me of this rhyme."

"Your dog looks like a frog?" His eyebrows crunched together.

I laughed and shook my head. "No, no, she's a greyhound. Her butt's so narrow that when she sits she does sit on what she ain't got almost, and her running is a lot like flying."

The pseudo smile returned. "Ah, a greyhound. Lovely dogs. Though I'd have thought exercising one sufficiently would be difficult in the city."

City? Willow Falls can hardly be called a city. Then I remembered the flea market was in High Cross. "Oh, I take her to the dog park most days to

2

run, and she's a total couch potato the rest of the time."

"How much is this?" demanded a blonde woman with dark roots and the face of a peevish hen. She held up a carved wooden frog brandishing a spear.

"That frog is three dollars," said the man.

She stared hard at it. "Okay. My boyfriend will like it." She dug into a large purple handbag and brought out three crumpled bills.

"Thank you, dear lady. I hope he enjoys it enormously." He turned back to me. "And will your boyfriend enjoy your chosen frog?" His tone was arch.

I looked down at the knickknack in my hand. About the size of my fist, it wore a Stetson hat and the tin star of an old-West sheriff. "I was thinking of my cousin's boyfriend. Is this your collection? Are you downsizing it or something?"

"Actually, I'm looking forward to a significant period of upsizing." He smiled as though at a private joke. "But yes, for the moment this is my frog collection."

"So does that make you the Frog Prince?" I ventured.

He laughed politely. "No, no, merely the—Frog Duke."

I nodded. "Just as well. Royalty doesn't seem to command much respect these days."

"Too true, poor dears. I suspect their behavior is not much different from their ancestors', but living in an age of instant and relentless communication has its costs."

3

"As do flea market frogs," I said. "If this one's reasonable, I'd better pay for it and get going, I've got a long drive and I've been here too long already."

"Yes, of course. Let's exchange a dollar for the look of the thing," he agreed. "Here, let me wrap that up for you."

He took the frog from my hand and bent to retrieve a sheet of newspaper and grocery bag from under the table. I fished in my fanny pack for some money, thinking that his pricing structure was curious, if he was charging me less for this frog than that other woman, whose frog was smaller and uglier.

Maybe he'd just enjoyed the conversation.

As I zipped the pack shut and looked up, I saw a familiar head of gray hair coming along the row of selling tables. So much for the anonymity of going to a flea market several towns away from home. The woman appeared to be focused on the various merchandise. Maybe if I hurried I could get away.

"I've got to be going." I threw the dollar bill on the table and reached for the bag.

He pulled it out of my reach and stared at me. What is with this guy? said the impatient voice in my head. Then, "Of course you do." He handed me the bag with the frog and picked up the bill from the table. "Let me only say how enormously I have enjoyed doing business with you."

"Um, any time." My repartee must have been more scintillating than I'd realized. "Good luck with the rest of the frogs." I turned toward the parking lot and took two hurrying steps before crashing into

4

someone.

"Oof!" was the woman's elegant response, and then a chilly, "Ah, Mrs. McGuire."

Straight into the lion's mouth. "Oh, hello, Mrs. Johnson. I beg your pardon, are you all right?" Trust me to bash into someone at least twenty years older than I and considerably smaller. This particular someone always made me feel as large as a haystack. At least I knew she already didn't like me, so I didn't have to worry about losing her regard.

She lifted a perfectly manicured hand to pat her gray hair. Nothing short of a hurricane—unusual in the Midwest—would be able to disarray those stiff locks. "No, no, I'm quite all right. Just a trifle warm. It looks as though we are in for a very hot summer."

I've never experienced a summer in this part of the country that wasn't scorching, but I had lived in Seattle for many years. Maybe they'd had some chilly ones here while I was gone. "I think you're right. Are you enjoying the flea market?"

She pursed her thin lips. "Quite pathetic, isn't it?" she sniffed. "One might as well go to—" she gave a small shudder— "a yard sale. Rows of tube socks and cheap jewelry. And useless junk like those frogs." She gestured toward the table I had just left.

I eased the bag I was holding behind my back. "I'm late for work," I said. "Kay is running the store alone this morning, so I'd better get going. Nice to see you."

"And you, dear." We gave each other equally insincere smiles before I started once more for the park-

5

ing lot.

"Where have you been? It's been crazy around here," my cousin Kay demanded. She perched on a tall stool behind the sales counter in her store, OKay Antiques, which gave her a good view around the shop. This was empty except for an ancient couple in the far corner going through a pile of vintage aprons.

"The flea market in High Cross," I said, dropping the package in my hand onto the counter. "I'm sure I told you I was going. It doesn't look crazy," I added, looking around the quiet room.

She planted her hands on her hips. "Yeah, *now* it's not. They all fled when they heard you coming. Seriously, twenty-seven people were in here ten minutes ago. You could have at least called me."

My expression must have given me away.

"Louisa, what did you do to your cell phone this time?"

"Nothing!" I protested.

"Nothing, huh. That means you either let the battery die or you set it down somewhere among your still unpacked possessions and can't find it."

I tried to change the subject. "I'm sorry, I know I'm late. You know how hard it is to rush through a flea market."

Her expression changed to eager. "Find anything good?"

"I scored a couple of Rookwood candle holders that I'm sure will sell—"

"Wow."

6

"Yeah, that's what I thought. And I found a really nice rolled leather collar for Jack. It's red." Jack is my friend Bob's low-slung black mutt, a Basset-Labrador mix with long velvety ears.

"He'll love it."

"Oh, and something I thought you might like to give Ed." I pointed to the package on the counter. "And I ran into a friend of yours, who said it used to be a good antiquing market but now it's just tube socks and cheap jewelry. She had a point. I think I'd already found all the good stuff."

Kay reached for the bag. "Who was that?"

"Ed's mother."

She froze with her hand midair. "Never, never refer to her as a friend of mine. I'm surprised you weren't struck down by lightning to even think such a thing."

I picked up the bag and tipped it over so that the wrapped contents rolled out. "Actually I ran into her literally. It's a wonder I didn't knock her down. She must be sturdier than she looks."

Her jaw dropped. "You ran over her with your *car*?" Her expression hovered between hope and horror.

A laugh burst out of me. "No, you ninny, I just walked into her. Geez."

"Oh." She had the grace to look relieved. Then she said, "Darn."

"May I trouble you for the time?" inquired a quavery voice from behind me.

I turned and saw the old man who'd been perusing

the linens. "Almost eleven," I told him. "Are you finding everything okay?"

His blue eyes twinkled. "My sister is enjoying herself enormously waxing nostalgic over those aprons. She is recalling a past that differs in significant respects from my own memories of the same period, but I think hers are better. I'm seriously considering switching over. Thank you for the time."

He turned and went back to the woman, who was beaming at a vintage hopsacking apron embroidered with cross stitch roosters. She said, "Elwood, remember that wonderful rooster plaque I made that mama hung in the kitchen? With all the different beans?"

I turned back to Kay, who said, "My mother had one of those bean roosters in our kitchen, remember?"

I nodded, smiling at the memory of my aunt.

Her eyes fell to the newspaper-wrapped lump lying on the counter. "What's this?" she asked, reaching for it.

"It's for you to give Ed, if you think he'd like it. I thought it was funny."

She ripped off the paper and pushed it aside, holding up the sheriff frog. "This is great," she said. "If I could get Ed into a Stetson, you'd hardly be able to tell them apart." She twisted the pot-bellied object in her hand to inspect it from various angles. It was cast of some kind of metal and gleamed softly in the overhead lights.

"It comes with an added benefit," I told her.

"Yeah? What?"

"I was in front of the booth with all the frogs when

I ran into Mrs. Johnson. She spoke disparagingly of them."

Kay's smile broadened. "Oh good, so there's every chance she'll hate this. Great! I'll give it to Ed tonight."

"I thought you'd like it. Let me go wash the flea market off my hands and then I'll take over the desk."

"Great," she said again, still looking at the frog. "Oh, Bob called. He's picking you up for dinner at seven."

"Did he say if he got my car taken care of?"

"Oh yeah, that. Yes, oil's changed, tires are rotated. How do you two remember which of your twin cars needs what?"

"He puts it on a calendar. My calendar has notations about birthdays and anniversaries, his tells him car things. It's all I can do to remember which one is my car." Our identical Civics were the cause of some amusement among our acquaintances, and were in fact the reason Bob and I had met, when I mistook his car for mine.

Kay held out the frog sheriff. "Here, take this guy back to my desk, would you? I don't want people swarming in off the street and trying to buy him."

"Sure," I said. I took the frog, then grabbed the discarded paper in which it had been wrapped. Something heavy fell, landed on my left big toe, and thudded to the floor. "Ow!" Startled by the pain of the impact, I dropped the frog sheriff, which smacked the top of my right foot, rolling in the other direction. "Ow! Shit!" I looked guiltily around, hoping no one had been offended.

"Ouch, that smarts," Kay said, leaning over the counter to peer at my feet. "What the heck was that?"

"Too bad I didn't have my garden boots on," I said, leaning down to pick up both missiles. "Sandals are not much protection."

"Louisa, you don't garden," my cousin reminded me.

Nature and I maintain an uneasy truce, the terms of which include my avoiding it as much as possible. "Yeah, but I bought some rubber boots for going to the dog park in the mornings. The grass is usually wet." I picked up the western frog, then snared the tissue-paper wrapped object that had fallen first. "There's another frog or something in here."

Putting the gift for Ed back on the counter, I felt the other lumpy bundle. It was decidedly heavy for its size, and well-padded with the wrapping material. I ripped away until I got to a layer secured with heavy tape. "Hand me the scissors," I said to Kay, who retrieved them from the drawer in front of her. I snipped and pulled away more packing, at last revealing another frog figurine.

I go to a lot of garage sales; unlike Mrs. Johnson I think it's really fun to poke through other people's stuff. And at those garage sales are many ugly knick-knacks, including a fair number of frogs.

This one was definitely in the running for the ugliest I've ever seen.

It appeared to be of some kind of plastic, though with a homemade quality. The color was a mottled olive streaked with yellow, and on its head was a yellow crown. The body was elongated, the crown was stumpy, and shallow bumps dotted the back.

"Wow, that is one awful frog," Kay said. We stared. She picked it up and turned it around as she had the sheriff frog. "It must be made of lead or something, it's really heavy."

"But it looks like plastic," I objected.

"Yeah. Weird."

"I wonder how it got in the bag," I said. "Could it have fallen in while he was wrapping up the other one? But could you accidentally bag something that heavy? I think it's just so ugly the guy figured throwing it in was the only way he'd ever get rid of it."

She looked at it again. "I could go there," she nodded. "Though if you squint and don't look at the color, the frog itself does have interesting lines. Except for the crown thingie."

I thought of part of my conversation with the man at the flea market and chuckled. "Maybe it's his calling card."

Kay gave me one of her "you're not making sense" looks. "Calling card?"

"The guy selling the frogs was English, and at some point in our conversation I said something about him being the frog prince. Maybe he keeps a supply of these and throws them in whenever he sells a frog, like a signature piece. Oh, wait, he said he wasn't the frog prince, he was the frog duke. How would you make a frog look like a duke?"

"I can't begin to imagine, nor why anyone would

want to." She held the ugly frog out to me. "Here, maybe you can use it for a door stop."

I took it, surprised again at its weight. "But I don't think I should keep it if it got in the bag accidentally."

"You're not going to turn around and drive back to the flea market to return it," Kay said flatly. "I need a potty break, and I'm betting those women looking in the window are going to come in and start asking a hundred questions."

I glanced over my shoulder. A group of five middle aged women were looking at the window display and arguing. "Right. Okay, let me take these to the office, and then you shall have the potty break of your dreams."

2

"Will you be having wine with your dinner?" The waiter held a pen over his order pad and looked down his nose at us.

Bob looked at me. "Glass or bottle?"

"Glass," I said, "or I'll fall asleep over the salad."

He nodded, knowing my early-to-bed-early-to-rise tendencies. "We'll have two glasses of the Sangiovese, and bring a plate of the risotto cakes with them. Thanks."

"Would you care to order your dinner now, or do you need a little more time?" Something about the way he pursed his lips told me that either choice would be wrong.

"Just the wine and appetizer for now, thanks." Bob's pleasant smile never wavered. The waiter contrived to look slightly tragic as he turned away.

Bob settled back in his chair and ran his hand over his graying brown hair. "I've got some news," he said.

Instantly something inside me froze. "Good news or bad news?"

"I *think* it's good news, at least I'm excited about it."

I thawed a little. "Go on, don't keep me in suspense," I urged.

"You remember that conference I went to in San Francisco back in February."

I nodded. "Yes, that period does stick in my mind." His trip to San Francisco had coincided with the temporary homelessness that made me agree to run a bed and breakfast for a few days. The few days turned out to include a snowstorm that stranded me on an island with a varied group of people and dogs, and ended with my being held at gunpoint by a mad counterfeiter in a house with a secret room. Bob also met a woman at the conference whose parents had left her a house in Willow Falls that I now owned. "What about it?"

"I got a call last week from one of the people who ran the conference," he said. Bob is a hypnotherapist whose main interest is hypnotic anesthesia. "They are starting a research project at Berkeley. He invited me to join the project, plus there's a good chance of my co-hosting a weekly radio show on therapeutic hypnotism."

"Wow! That's fantastic," I said. "You're going to be a star!"

The laugh lines around his nice hazel eyes crinkled. "Right. Next stop Hollywood." Then he sobered. "I'm really interested in this, both the research and the radio thing. But—"

"Here you are," the waiter said, lifting a wine glass off a tray and setting it in front of me. "And for you, sir—" Bob's wine was delivered, "—and some tasty little risotto cakes with our special roasted tomato cream confit." He moved aside the vase of yellow alstromeria blossoms and deposited the plate on the center of the table. "Are you ready to order dinner?"

Neither of us had so much as glanced at the menu. "Give us a few more minutes," Bob suggested. The waiter sniffed and drooped away. Bob picked up his menu, but didn't open it.

"But what?" He looked at me questioningly. "You said you're interested in this, but."

He put down the menu again. "Right. I do find the whole thing very exciting, but...but it means moving to California. Which is not something I ever imagined I would do." He looked very serious. The idea of moving to California can have that effect. "But—there's that word again—I'm hoping you'll come with me."

"What?"

He reached across the table for my hand. His was warm and smooth, and he held my fingers with just the right amount of pressure. "I want you to come with me." His eyes lit up. "We could live in Berkeley, or San Francisco, or wherever you like. Just think, Louisa, what a great time we'd have. I'll be working quite a lot, but you've told me you like the Bay Area."

I fell back in my chair, but left my hand in his. "I—I don't know what to say."

"You could leave behind the heat and humidity of

the summers here, not to mention the winter snow. It will be great."

"Yes, but—but I've just moved into a new house."

"We could find someone to rent it."

"I haven't even unpacked half my stuff yet."

"Easy to put into storage then. The dogs would love it. We could take them to the beach."

I had a feeling that Emily Ann would consider beach sand nothing more than annoying grit between her toes. He must have seen my doubt.

"Don't say anything yet." He gave my fingers a squeeze, then let go of my hand and opened his menu. "Take as long as you need to think about it. Should we order dinner?"

I picked up my menu, though I knew it was the same as the last umpty times I'd been here. I tried to think of something I wanted to eat, but nothing came to mind. I laid down the menu again. "When is all this happening?"

His wide mouth spread in a humorous grimace. "Ah. Pretty fast, actually. Both projects are starting soon."

"How fast, how soon?"

"I'm flying on Monday."

"Monday?" It came out a squeak. "This Monday?"

He nodded. "I'm booked on an 8:30 flight out of High Cross."

"Bob! I expected to hear 'next month' or 'September.' Monday?" I still wasn't sure I'd heard him correctly.

He looked embarrassed. "They made the reserva-

16

tion, but if you can come I'm sure I can get another ticket."

An image of Kay's outraged face swam into my head. "I can't possibly desert Kay without any notice," I said. "She needs more help in the store, not less."

"Of course," he said quickly. He was probably seeing his own version of Kay's outraged face.

"I know it's a cliché, but this is awfully sudden."

"I'm sorry to spring it on you. I haven't been hiding it from you for months or anything. Someone dropped out of the Berkeley project at the last minute, and they thought of me."

I felt a little mollified. "Of course they did. You're good at this stuff."

"That's what I get for agreeing to speak at that conference when what's his name couldn't attend—a reputation as a pinch hitter."

"Or a reputation as someone who knows his stuff. Anyway, isn't there some saying about success being able to grab an opportunity when it comes? This really is exciting."

"Anyway, it's a trial run on both sides. I haven't signed any contracts yet."

The waiter reappeared at Bob's elbow. He noticed our untouched food. In hushed tones he asked, "Is something wrong with the risotto cakes?"

I managed a smile. "I'm sure they're fine." I realized my throat was feeling tight, far too tight to encompass food. "Actually, if you don't mind, Bob, I think I'd like to go home."

"Are you sure? I know you like that pasta dish

here."

"I—I'm not really hungry."

He gave a quick nod, pulled out his wallet, and handed some money to the waiter. In a few minutes we were in his little Honda, pulling out of the parking lot. The evening was almost as warm as the morning had been, and I turned the fan for the air conditioner to high.

I could think of nothing to say. My mind was completely blank, a white screen. My feelings seemed frozen and blank as well. I wondered how I was going to feel about Bob's news when I thawed. I liked him very, very much—but my disastrous marriage had made me cautious about taking our relationship to any deeper level. Going with him to California would be way more serious than taking a trip together, or sharing Jack.

We drove up the hill past the pond that used to be a limestone quarry, about half a mile from my driveway. Bob broke the silence. "I really botched telling you about this."

I shook my head. "No, no, it's just..." My voice trailed off. I tried again. "I just need some time to think about things and figure out how I feel."

"Of course. Take all the time you need."

"Are you—are you staying here tonight?" I glanced over at him just as he gave me a quick look. He flicked on the turn signal and turned into my drive, winding between trees toward the house.

"I wish I could, but I can't. I've got a lot to do before Monday. Not just packing, I've got to notify my appointments that I won't be able to see them. I feel really guilty about them, and you. I'll be able to refer them, but still. I wish you would come with me. I feel like I'm deserting you."

Did I feel deserted? I tried to probe my emotions, but they were still hiding. "Do you want me to take you to the airport?" A little movie starring myself spun behind my eyes. I bravely watched his plane take off, my head held high as a gentle breeze stirred my hair. A single tear coursed down my cheek, which I caught on the tip of a finger before turning away, the jet disappearing overhead. I blinked, and came back to the present.

Bob parked neatly beside my car and pulled up the hand brake before switching off the engine. "I'd love a ride," he said. "I hardly dared to ask. Could I— I'd like to leave a couple of things here for now. Until I figure out what I'm doing." I nodded, and he went on. "Is it okay to leave my car with you?"

"Sure," I said. "I can drive it every few days. What else?"

"Will you keep Jack for a while?"

Jack. Bob's dog. Jack, who stayed with me and Emily Ann even more often than Bob did. Who had saved my life twice. At the thought of Bob taking Jack to Berkeley, my throat constricted. I croaked, "Of course leave him. We love him."

Bob smiled warmly at me. "And he certainly loves you. Come on, let's get you inside. I'm sorry dinner was a bust."

I shook my head. "Not a problem. Do you want something to eat?" I opened the car door and stepped out.

Bob followed me to the front door, saying, "No thanks, I'm fine. I'll make a sandwich when I get to the condo and eat it while I start a list of what I need to do."

"Efficient," I nodded, putting the key in the door lock. Bob moved close behind me and put his hands on my shoulders. After a moment I leaned back against him. I felt him kiss the top of my head, then his arms circled me.

"Oh, Louisa, I am so going to miss you," he said. "Maybe this is a huge mistake. What was I thinking?"

"No, you should do it. At least try it. You owe that to yourself."

"Promise you'll think about going with me."

I nodded. The single tear rolled down my cheek for real.

3

I arrived at the dog park the next morning later than usual. The sun shone bright and my head ached. I'd spent the night in fruitless thought that finally abated enough to allow sleep at about four a.m.

Several dogs ran after balls or wrestled with each other within the chain link fence. I opened the gate and entered, quickly unclipping Emily Ann's leash. A swirl of dogs ran by, and Emily Ann took off and led the pack across the field. Her long legs covered the ground with effortless grace. The poetry of a greyhound in motion always has the power to bring a sting to my eyes.

"Hey! Louisa! You're just the person I wanted."

I turned away from the dogs toward Dan, another dog park regular, steaming my way. His dog Roxie trailed behind him, pausing to sniff an intriguing clump of grass along the way.

"Hi, Dan," I croaked. I hadn't spoken yet that morning and my voice came out sounding like it had not gotten enough sleep. Fair enough.

He stopped beside me. His brow wrinkled. His

nice brown eyes were on a level with mine. "You okay?"

I wanted to blurt out that Bob was moving to California, but I knew if I did the news would reach Kay before I could tell her myself. The grapevine has always flourished in Willow Falls, and cell phones have added only a little to its speed. So I nodded. "I'm fine. Just didn't sleep much last night."

He pulled out a purple bandana and wiped his face. "Too hot," he agreed. "Roxie actually slept on the bathroom floor instead of the foot of the bed." He looked down at the big brown shepherd, collapsed at his feet, panting. "A night on the tiles, huh, Rox?" She looked up at him and thumped her tail. He turned back to me. "Barb had an idea for the auction next week."

"Oh, good. What was it?" In the years I had been in Seattle, a dedicated group of volunteers had gotten the city council to donate this former ball field for a dog park by promising to finance its upkeep. The dog park fundraising auction was the biggest topic of conversation in town these days, and not just at the dog park. "I can hardly wait to see this auction. Kay used to tell me about it every year. Though I don't know how you could possibly top last year."

"Oh, we will." He bounced on the balls of his feet. "You're gonna love this. She saw this thing on TV—" He stopped, looking at something over my shoulder. I turned. A woman had just entered the gate with a dog.

The dog was a dainty dark brown miniature poodle, immaculately groomed, sporting a bright red ribbon on the top of each ear. It raised its feet high above the wet grass with each step, making the jewels on its collar and leash glitter in the sunlight.

The woman accompanying the poodle was equally groomed. Her gray hair was molded about her head in stiff swirls, and she wore a light beige short sleeved jacket belted over matching slacks. Her shoes had the subtly gleaming leather and precisely correct heel height of really expensive footwear. When she leaned over to unclip the leash from her dog a silk scarf shone around her neck.

"Oh, no," I breathed.

The dozen or so dogs running loose in the field noticed the newcomers and careened over to say hello. Fortunately it was a mild crew that morning and they merely circled around the woman and dog, sniffing and panting, before charging off again. The poodle went with them.

"Henri!" the woman called. "Prince Henri, come back here!"

The dog didn't bat an ear. He was very fast, and dashed in a big circle with the other dogs. Halfway across the field he suddenly stopped and squatted. Then he charged off again, grabbed a tennis ball from Marley the retriever, and sprinted away.

His owner still stood near the gate, making no move to go over and clean up after her dog, which is an iron-clad rule at the dog park.

"Maybe she didn't notice that her dog pooped," Dan suggested.

"I'm not going to tell her," I said. "Don't you know

who she is?'

Dan shook his head.

"Mrs. Johnson," I muttered darkly.

"Mrs. Johnson? Mrs. Johnson as in Ed's mother?"

I nodded. "That's the one."

"I never knew she had a dog."

"I'm sure she didn't. Kay would have said." Kay loves dogs as much as I do. If a dog had been at Ed's house—his mother lived with him and his daughter—I would have heard about it.

"Trudy over at the Cut 'n' Curl told my wife Mildred that Mrs. Johnson hates your cousin more than poison."

"Don't mention Mrs. Johnson, Kay and poison in one breath," I warned.

Mrs. Johnson remained where she was, watching her dog with an anxious expression as the poodle led the pack on a zigzag course around the field.

"She is pretty scary looking," Dan said, squinting over at her.

"Nah, just over dressed. She actually looks deceptively mild. It's when you get to know her she's scary."

"Still, she needs to pick up after her dog."

We looked at each other. Dan shrugged.

"Okay, I'll tell her," he said. He headed toward the newcomer. Roxie surged to her feet and trotted after him. "Good morning!" I heard him call. Mrs. Johnson started, as though she hadn't noticed that other people were around. Perhaps she assumed that dogs brought themselves to the park, or had a limo service that picked them up.

I was too far away to hear their conversation, but gestures and expressions told the story. Dan began with a smile, probably introducing himself, then pointed in the direction that the poodle had availed himself of the facilities. Mrs. Johnson's mouth thinned into a line. She inclined her head in a regal way, spoke briefly, and started off across the field. Dan and Roxie ambled back to stand beside me again.

"That went okay," he reported.

"Good. She's usually polite. It's just knowing how much she hates my cousin that's so creepy. So what did Barb see on TV?"

His eyes lit up in amusement. "Oh, yeah. Well, they had these dogs that—"

Halfway to her destination Mrs. Johnson bent down and picked up a couple of maple leaves that had blown onto the field from some nearby trees.

"Oh, good heavens. The woman didn't bring any plastic bags."

Dan turned to look. We watched Mrs. Johnson inspect the ground, clutching those leaves. She was nowhere near what she was looking for, and it wasn't something that could be handled with a couple of maple leaves.

"I can't stand this," I said.

I walked quickly across the field before I lost my nerve. When I got close enough to speak rather than yell I said, "Good morning. Did you forget your plastic bags? Here, I have some extras." I pretended to smile as I held one out to her.

She started. "Oh, Mrs. McGuire, I didn't realize

25

you were here. Um, thank you, I—I have never had a dog before." She took the bag I proffered as though it might turn into a rattlesnake in her hand.

"No problem. I always carry extra bags. You never know when they'll come in handy. I think your dog—Prince Henri, is that his name?—went over here a little farther."

We walked another twenty feet together, watching the ground carefully. I spotted Henri's output and pointed to it with my foot. "Here you go."

Mrs. Johnson's expression of grim horror and the white knuckles of the hand still holding the bejeweled leash made it clear she was telling the truth about never having a dog before. I stifled a sigh, annoyed at my ability to feel sorry for absolutely anyone.

"Okay, here's the easy way," I told her. "Put a plastic bag over your hand, pick up the poop, then pull the bag over it and you're done." I demonstrated. The effluvium of a small poodle was miniscule compared to that of a greyhound, and I was deft from much practice.

"Oh...I see. Thank you." She was pale under her stern expression.

"You can get bags at the pet store that have a sort of wire frame and a cardboard handle," I went on. "Some people like them because they keep you further from the, um, product, but lots of us just reuse all our plastic bags this way. It's not a bad idea to carry some of those little hand wipes in your fanny pack. I'll throw this away in the can by the gate. Emily Ann and I were just leaving. Have a nice morning."

She opened her mouth to say something—I like to think to thank me, but wouldn't have bet the farm on it—but just then the pack of dogs surged by. Prince Henri was leading them on a grand run. He jumped up on his owner a couple of times, then dashed in a circle around us before careening away. The previously perfectly-brushed coat was soaked with dew and plastered to his body, the wet hair on his ears hanging down in dreadlocks. One of the ribbons was gone and the other was untied and had turned from red to muddy gray. The jeweled collar was liberally streaked with dirt. I could tell from his happy grin that Prince Henri was having a wonderful time.

Next to me, Mrs. Johnson moaned. I looked over at her. Her beautiful slacks had muddy dog prints on them, and her lips trembled as she watched Prince Henri running with his new friends. She seemed unable to speak.

"Don't worry," I told her cheerfully, "Prince Henri will clean up in no time. He'll be worn out from all this exercise, and you can pop him into the sink for a little bath and then brush him and he'll sleep all afternoon. See you later."

I hurried back to Dan, looking for Emily Ann as I went. I spotted her with a lanky black and white mutt named Elvis, taking turns sniffing some bushes. "Emily Ann!" I called. "Let's go!" Her head came up, and she loped toward me. We arrived next to Dan at the same time.

"Mission accomplished?" he asked.

I nodded. "Life is strange, isn't it? I'd have made

book that she would be the last person I'd ever give poop-scooping lessons to. Listen, we've got to go. I'm meeting Kay for breakfast. Can I catch you later on Barb's idea?"

"Sure," he agreed. "You probably need a nice cup of tea to steady your nerves. I'll see you tomorrow."

"Same time, same place," I agreed, clipping Emily Ann's leash to her collar. I walked with my dog to the gate, depositing the plastic bag of poodle droppings in the trash can on the way. As I closed the gate behind us, I saw Mrs. Johnson standing, still alone, where I had left her. Her shoulders drooped, and she looked elderly and a bit forlorn as she watched her little dog tearing about the field.

Kay was already in our usual booth at the Bluebird Cafe, the last one to the left of the door. I could tell from the shine in her ashy brown hair over the back of the booth that she'd had it colored that week. She was reading the High Cross paper and sipping coffee from a heavy white mug.

"Hey," I said, sliding into the seat across from her.

She looked up and smiled at me. "Hey! Dorothy's making raspberry pancakes this morning."

"Yummers, sounds good. Been here long?"

"Nah, still on the first cup," she said, picking up her mug and sipping. "Did you just get up?"

"Why? Didn't I comb my hair or something?"

"Just wondered, you're usually here before me. Did you comb your hair?"

"I think so, but it probably got mussed from standing on end. I just saw Mrs. Johnson at the dog park."

Her mug thunked onto the table. "At the *dog* park? Ed's mother? What in the world was she doing there?"

"Exercising her dog. I had to show her how to pick up after it."

She stared at me. "Mrs. Johnson doesn't have a dog."

"She does now. A poodle. Prince Henri."

"No!"

"Yes. And you haven't lived until you've seen Mrs. Johnson looking for dog poop armed only with a couple of maple leaves. Apparently she didn't know you have to pick up after your dog."

"No!"

"Yup."

"A *maple* leaf? Man, I am going to have to start coming to the dog park, you have all the fun."

"Two maple leaves, and you are most welcome to come with us any morning. The fun can be all yours next time."

"Hey, Louisa." Cleta, our favorite waitress, placed a china teapot decorated with bluebirds, then a cup and saucer in front of me. "Yesterday hot enough for ya? I could have stayed in Texas if I wanted to roast in May, you know?"

"Thanks, Cleta," I said, pulling the cup toward me. "I know, it was awful, wasn't it? I hate to think what July will be like."

"Y'all decided what you want this mornin'?"

29

"Pancakes," we said in unison, then grinned at each other and hooked pinkies.

"All righty then. Dorothy made up some fresh orange syrup, or you can have the regular maple syrup. Or both." She looked at us. "Right, both."

She headed back toward the kitchen, pausing briefly to clear a few dishes from a table and steer a couple of tourists standing at the door into seats. I lifted the lid on my teapot and stirred the contents gently, then poured a cup, adding a bit of sugar and cream. The first sip was perfect.

Kay folded the newspaper. Something caught her eye and she paused to read. With her eyes still on the paper, she asked, "How's Bob? Nice dinner last night?"

I opened my mouth to reply, but my throat closed. Took a deep breath and tried again. "He's—he's going to California."

Her eyes still on the paper, she said, "Oh, that's nice. Another conference? How long this time?"

"Maybe forever."

Something in my tone got through. Her head came up. "What?"

I told her about the research project and radio show that were luring Bob to the West Coast, then added, "He wants me to go with him."

She slumped back in her seat. "Well, damn. Now I will have to look for someone else to work in the store."

"You need to do that anyway, but I didn't say I was going. Are you firing me?"

She sat up again. "You're not going? What do you

mean you're not going?"

I couldn't help sighing, remembering the sleepless night I had just spent thinking, thinking, thinking. "I haven't decided."

"But I thought you loved the guy."

Cleta returned to our table to drop off a bowl of softened butter and two mismatched china cream pitchers filled with warm syrups. Part of the fun of the Bluebird is seeing which plate or cup you get that day. I recognized one as a piece I'd bought at a garage sale and given to the café. "Pancakes will be out in a minute," she said, and hurried away.

I dipped the tip of my spoon into the orange syrup and tasted it. Fresh juice and grated peel warmed my mouth. "Mmm, This should be good."

"Don't change the subject," Kay ordered. "Are you going to California or not?"

I shook my head. "I don't know. It's not something I can decide in a minute, and I only heard about it last night."

Her eyebrows drew together. "Of course you can decide in a minute if it's what you want to do. And what do you mean you only heard about it last night? Do you mean Bob decided to move to Berkeley without even asking your opinion?"

I stared at her. This had not occurred to me. "Um, yeah. But he said he's just trying it out. He hasn't signed any contracts."

"I can't believe it! Who does he think he is?"

"What?" I could see that she was getting angry.

"That just burns my buns, Louisa. I thought better

31

of Bob. This is high handed and arrogant and I do not like to see you treated this way. I've got half a mind to call him right now and tell him what I think of him. In fact that's exactly what I'm going to do." She grabbed her purse from the seat beside her and yanked it open, groping inside and pulling out a tiny red cell phone.

"Wait," I said as she flipped it open. "You don't need to do that."

She ignored me and punched a couple of buttons. Bob was saved by the arrival of Cleta with two large plates of steaming pancakes. Cleta frowned at Kay.

"All right, young lady, you just put that thing away," she told my cousin. "This is a café, not a phone booth, and Louisa deserves more courtesy from you than to have to watch you talking to somebody else."

"Louisa needs someone to tell Bob a thing or two," Kay retorted.

"No I don't."

Cleta set down our plates and reached out her hand for the phone. "Louisa is perfectly able to handle Bob however she sees fit."

Kay scowled, but handed over the phone. Cleta is not above taking your food away if she is displeased with you. Cleta nodded her approval and placed our breakfasts on the table.

"That's better. I'm sure whatever it is can wait. You may have your phone back when you leave. Now eat your nice pancakes. I'll bring you more coffee in a minute. Louisa, do you need more hot water in that pot?"

"No, ma'am," I said.

"All righty, then," she said, and was gone.

Kay and I looked at each other. We began to laugh. "She's got us well trained," I said.

Kay reached for the butter. "Too right. Some things you just don't mess with. Cleta with a plate of food is one of them."

We busied ourselves with butter and syrup pitchers. The first bite was nirvana, comfort food of the highest order. I concentrated on eating, letting the tartness of raspberries and sweet citrus syrup form a barrier to unwanted thoughts. After a few minutes, Kay spoke again.

"Okay, I'm sorry about going off halfcocked. I won't call Bob and yell at him, or not yet anyway. But don't you want to be with him?"

I sighed. "Yes. No. I don't know. I like him a lot. Okay, okay, I guess I—I do love him. I'm not sure I even know what that means. But I've told you all along, I don't want to get married again. I really like living by myself. I'm happy when I'm with Bob, but I'm perfectly fine when I'm not."

"That sounds healthy," she admitted. "But not being with him because he's in High Cross is different from not being with him because he's on the West Coast. I think you're going to miss his, um, companionship more than you think." She waggled her eyebrows at me.

"Okay, maybe." This wasn't a conversation I wanted to have, especially in public. "But that's not the only thing I'm going to miss."

"What do you mean?"

"Who the heck is going to mow my grass?"

She snorted a laugh. "Good point. Boyfriends are easier to find than good yard help." She cut another piece of pancake and put it in her mouth, chewing vigorously.

"Maybe I could pay Bob to stay here. How much do people get paid to mow these days?"

"Louisa, I live over my store. How should I know? How much are they offering him?"

"He didn't say," I admitted, "but he's not doing it for the money. At least I don't think he is. I guess I'll have to do the mowing myself. Thank heavens most of the property is wooded. If I had to mow five acres I'd just lie down and die."

"Or maybe buy a tractor," Kay suggested. "I said you should get a riding mower instead of that push thing."

"Bob didn't want a riding mower. He said he needed the exercise he'd get mowing my grass."

She grinned wickedly at me.

"No, that is *not* a euphemism. Behave yourself." I can read her like a book.

Cleta appeared with a carafe of steaming coffee. "Pancakes okay?" she asked, filling Kay's mug. We both nodded.

"Wonderful. Perfect," I said. She patted my shoulder, then headed along the row of booths, filling cups as she went.

I decided it was time for a change of subject. "Did you give the frog to Ed last night?"

"No, he was on duty. We're supposed to go out to-

34

night. I'll give it to him then. Did you throw away the other one?"

I had forgotten all about the extra frog. "No. At least I don't think I did. I haven't thought about anything other than Bob and California since last night. What the heck did I do with it?" I closed my eyes, trying to recreate the previous day's movements in my mind. "I was in a hurry because I needed to grab a shower before Bob arrived." I could see myself unlocking the front door, climbing the circular stairs, kicking off my shoes, turning on the shower. I had no image of handling an ugly frog.

I opened my eyes. "Nope. No idea what became of it."

She shook her head. "Louisa, you do that all the time. I guess losing a frog makes a change from losing a phone. You should check the pockets of whatever you were wearing."

"Kay, I am not two years old. Of course I'll check my pockets." If I remembered.

"I'm sure it'll turn up. Or you could just leave it lost. It was ugly."

"I know. But I still feel odd about having it. If I knew the guy didn't want it I could throw it away, or give it to Dan for the auction or something."

"Well, I had a thought," Kay said. "I was looking at the sheriff frog last night, and I remembered that I know someone on the organizing committee for that flea market. Do you remember Joan Stillman?"

I shook my head.

"Probably not, she's a couple of years younger

35

than me so your paths wouldn't have crossed in school, and she was the mousiest little thing. She married an accountant in his thirties right after she graduated and divorced him a couple of years later, then moved to Chicago for several years. About five years ago she moved back. She'd had a boob job and done something to her teeth and gone blonde. Not long after she came back she married one of the associate pastors at that church in High Cross that has the flea market." Kay always knows everything about everyone.

"And what does her boob job have to do with my ugly frog?"

"Nothing. I was just telling you who she is."

"So boobs aside, who is she?"

Kay frowned at me. "I told you. She's on the committee that runs the flea market."

"So?"

"So she may be able to tell us who the guy was who sold you the sheriff frog, and you could get in touch with him to see if he meant to give you the ugly one. You seemed concerned about it yesterday." She picked up her coffee and sipped, glaring over the rim of the mug.

I gave her a grateful smile. "What a good idea! Thanks. If I can find the darned thing again I'll know whether I can toss it with a clear conscience."

"We can call her from the shop after breakfast. I've got her number in my computer."

I glanced at my watch. "Won't she still be in church? Don't pastor's wives always attend?"

"They get special dispensation the day after

36

they've run a flea market. The real question is, will she be up yet."

4

My hand shook a little as I inserted the key into the padlock. The lock snapped open with a click. I removed the key from the door and slid it back into my jeans pocket. Taking a deep breath of early morning air, I pulled open the shed door.

A quick check for spiders—none, good—and my fear subsided, but my loathing increased. I gritted my teeth as I stared down at the object before me. I wanted to slam the door and jump into my car and drive away, perhaps never to return.

"Not very practical," said a snotty voice in my head. "Recreating *Thelma and Louise* with Jack and Emily Ann for your sidekicks would be something of an over-reaction and you know it."

"How about the *Wizard of Oz* instead?" I replied

aloud. "We could ask the wizard for—oh!" Jack, drawn by my voice and no doubt assuming I was talking to him, had come up behind me and touched the back of my hand with his cold wet nose. "Jack, you startled me."

He wagged happily, always glad to be of service.

"What do you think, should we go look for the yellow brick road?"

I shouldn't have said 'go' aloud. He began to make big bucking circles. Emily Ann lay in the shade of a tree a few feet away, watching him with an air of patient tolerance.

"Sorry, Jack, not right now. I have to take care of this first." I turned back to the shed, squared my shoulders in steely resignation, gripped horizontal rubbered handles and pulled. The lawnmower rattled out of the shed.

When I bought my house, mounds of snow had created a dazzlingly white landscape. I knew the house came with about five acres of land, much of it wooded. The actual yard around the house seemed minimal; some pleasant arches of cleared space among the trees in which to enjoy the outdoors. Bob assured me he'd be happy to help with yard work, that it helped him relax and was a good way to get some exercise.

But Bob had left for California yesterday morning. As soon as I left him at the airport, I wondered if I had made a terrible mistake not being on the plane with him. I'd gone home, locked myself in with the dogs, and watched sappy romantic movies all day and into the evening.

I woke on Tuesday at my usual early hour, determined to buck up and get on with things. I needed to be at the shop at ten, and I intended to mow my grass before I left the house.

Kay's father, my Uncle Bill, had taught us both how to run a power mower when we were in junior high. The three of us had taken turns mowing their lawn, nursing glasses of icy lemonade in the shade of a huge elm tree between passes with the mower. We'd learned to hand off the mower to the next person like a relay racer handing off the baton, and we always finished the job with a run through the sprinkler to cool off, even though Kay and I were far too old and sophisticated by then to run through sprinklers.

But junior high was a long time ago, and I hadn't mowed a lawn in years. My husband had hired a pricey lawn service to take care of the property in Seattle, and my parents had paid a neighbor to cut their grass when he did his own. I'd made the same arrangement with the neighbor until I sold their place and bought this one. And now this yard needed a trim, and no handy neighbor in sight.

Briefly I considered calling the guy to see if he'd schlep his mower across town to my new house. But then I remembered he was 83 years old and no longer owned a car.

So probably not.

Before I came out I had looked in my filing cabinet for any instructions that might have come with the mower. Nothing. Perhaps Bob had taken the owner's manual home with him when we bought the mower and it was somewhere in his files. I was on my own with this machine. My loathing increased.

I bent over the mower, grabbed the starter rope, and yanked. The blades whirred, the rope snapped back, and the machine sat silent. I tried again, pulling harder. Same result, or non-result. I straightened, glaring at the mower, then took a deep breath. I braced one foot on the top, grabbed the rope, and pulled as hard and fast as I could. It snapped out of my hand and reeled back into the engine, and I lost my balance and fell onto my butt. My tailbone landed on a rock. Pain shot up my spine.

Hot tears sprang to my eyes. "Damn you, Bob," I sobbed, letting the tears fall. Jack rushed over to give me a couple of consoling kisses. Emily Ann joined us and settled beside me, resting her head on my knee. I cried for a few minutes, then wiped my face with the back of my hand.

"I don't know how to start this damned thing," I told the dogs. I gave a final sniff. "Furthermore, I do not want to know how to start this damned thing. I hate doing stuff that makes me all hot and sweaty." I paused, thinking of one or two exceptions to that rule. "Okay, I hate most things that make me hot and sweaty," I admitted. Jack thumped his tail. He appreciates the finer shades of truth. "Maybe we should just let this grass grow. We could have a meadow instead of a lawn. Come on, let's go to the dog park."

Jack began to buck and whirl once more.

At the park, Dan pounced as soon as I'd loosed Emily Ann and Jack and they dashed away to meet their friends. "We need more donations for the auction," he said urgently.

"Okay," I nodded. "I'm sure I can find some stuff, and I'll hold up Kay for a donation too. Does it need to be really good stuff or can you use gag items?"

"Both, especially if the gag items are weird enough. People get into the spirit of the thing and lose their heads and it's all gravy for us."

"Or Gravy Train," I agreed. "I've got this frog that is definitely weird enough. If I can find it. I think I carried it in from my car but I've lost track of it. And if it doesn't turn out to really belong to someone else."

"Sounds complicated for a frog."

"Oh, it is. Definitely."

"Someone was asking about you yesterday," Dan went on. His eyes strayed to a young Lab puppy that was bumbling in an adorable way after his dog Roxie.

"Me? Who was it?" As long as it wasn't a reporter. I'd had enough of them in the past year.

Dan shrugged. "Just some woman. I didn't talk to her myself. Bethie mentioned it."

"But what did she want?"

"I think she was asking about Emily Ann," he said. "Bethie said she was looking for someone with a greyhound." Roxie paused in her perambulation across the field and the pup ran into her. We could almost hear her long-suffering sigh from where we stood.

"Poor Roxie," I laughed, "it's hard having an entourage. Maybe it was someone who's been thinking about getting a greyhound and wanted to know more about them."

Dan nodded. "Could be. Not many greyhounds around here; Emily Ann's the only one that comes to the park."

Jack and Emily Ann were on the far side of the park now with several other dogs. Some scent had several noses riveted to the ground.

"If she comes back tell her she definitely should get a greyhound. Emily Ann's been great. What did she look like?"

Dan shook his head. "No idea. But—" he paused to look around at the other groups of dog owners across the field. "—yes, there's Bethie with George and Con-suela. You could ask her." He glanced back to see what his dog was doing, and shook his head. The lab pup was in a play bow, gnawing on Roxie's ankle. The shepherd gazed down at the infant with loathing. "I'd better go rescue Rox. She'll let a puppy rip her up before she'll tell it to stop."

We headed in our separate directions. I glanced at my watch and realized I needed to hurry or I'd be late at the store again.

"Hi!" I called to the chatting group. They turned to me, smiling. "Bethie, Dan said someone was asking for me?"

"Hi, Louisa." Bethie was in her early twenties, a blonde Amazon who wore bike shorts all year round. Her dog Foo, a pale yellow Pekingese, believed with all his heart that he owned the world. "Yeah, it was yes-terday I think. Or maybe the day before. No, yesterday. I remember because that was the day Gina Torelli's little boy Conrad finally did a somersault on the mat."

Bethie put young children through their paces at a kinder-gym. I didn't see any connection between a somersault and someone asking about greyhounds, but since I'd talked to Bethie before I knew better than to ask. "Who was she, do you know?"

"Who, Gina Torelli? She was a Baumschmidt before she married."

"No, the woman who was asking about greyhounds."

"Oh, her. Dunno. Never saw her before. She was standing outside the fence watching the dogs when I got here, and she asked me if any greyhounds ever came here. So I said sure, Emily Ann, and she asked me who owned her, so I told her it's you. And I brought Foo on in and he pooped so I picked up after him and when I turned around to throw the bag away she was gone."

"What did she look like?"

Bethie shrugged and spread out her hands. "I dunno, just a person. Older. Brown hair with some gray in it. Not very good muscle tone, and she could use some ab work. I only looked at her for a second. She didn't have a dog with her."

Except for the lack of dog, Bethie's description could apply to myself and about a third of the women in Willow Falls. "Thanks. If you see her again ask her what she wants. If she was thinking about adopting a greyhound I'd want to encourage her. They really are

44

great dogs."

"Emily Ann sure is," Bethie agreed. Blonde amazons can be quite sweet.

5

"Good afternoon, this is OKay Antiques," I said into the phone. Mentally I readied my stock answers to the usual questions about hours and inventory.

"Oh, hi, is this Kay?" a woman's voice came down the line.

"I'm sorry, Kay is busy with a customer," I replied, glancing across the room. Kay was charming a collector from Nashville who looked ready to buy out the store. "This is Louisa. Can I help you with something, or may I take a message?"

"I'm calling her back, she left a message on my machine Sunday," the woman said. "I've been out of town since Saturday evening. This is Joanie Stillman. Could you tell her I called?"

The name seemed familiar. I pulled a pad of paper closer to write it down. "Joanie Stillman," I repeated, then realized who she was. "Oh, Mrs. Stillman, I know why Kay called you. We wanted to ask you something about the flea market your church ran last weekend."

She laughed. "That thing. Well, if you called to ask me if your church should start one, my answer is no. Find some other fund raiser. Rob a bank or kidnap a millionaire, or start making personalized hot air balloons. Just don't have a flea market."

"Goodness. Not a happy experience."

"Oh, I'm exaggerating, of course. It's always a lot of work but it's fun too. But this year was just crazy from beginning to end."

"Why? What happened?"

"Honey, what didn't happen? First the woman chairing the committee was transferred by her job to another state and left in a hurry, so I had to take over. Which apparently gave some other people the idea that leaving town was the way to get out of working on this thing, and two more up and moved. Then the woman assigned to booth registrations suddenly decided to marry a widower with three young children and resigned to take care of them. Then the publicity chair fell out of a tree and broke an arm and a leg."

"Good grief!" I exclaimed.

"You said it," she agreed. "So a planning committee of ten people was suddenly a committee of five people, and nobody else wanted to come and play."

"I think I'd have left town too," I admitted.

"It did cross my mind," she said. "And that was only the stuff leading up to the day."

"What happened on the day?" I looked across at Kay once more, who caught my eye. She raised an

47

eyebrow. I gave a little shake of my head and pointed to myself, and she gave an equally small nod, and returned her attention to the teapot her customer was holding. "I know it was awfully hot. I was there early and it was already roasting."

"You came to the market? Great! Wish I'd known, I'd have said hi. I remember you from school. You were a lofty senior when I was a freshman, and I couldn't imagine I'd ever be that grown up myself."

I smiled, thinking of myself at that age. "If it's any comfort, I've never been that grown up since."

She laughed. "Don't I know it. I've got a nephew that age, and he's too cool for words. I made him help me on Saturday and it just about killed him."

"So what did happen?" I asked again. The bell on the door tinkled, and a young couple entered with a child of about three. They began to browse, and the child struck off on her own, heading for a table set with a display of Staffordshire figurines. "Uh oh, we might be moments from disaster here too, Joan. Could you hang on?"

"What's wrong?"

"Small child, inattentive parents, china," I recited.

"Call me back later," she said. "I should be around for the rest of the day. Bye!"

Hanging up the phone, I turned to Jack, who was curled on his cushion behind the counter. "Jack!" I called softly. His head came up with the big ears cocked. "Child alert!"

Jack jumped to his feet wagging, and I led him over to the little girl. He deftly inserted himself between her and the table of china.

"Doggie!" she cried, patting his back. He wagged at her, then moved slowly to an open aisle, where he flopped down. The child followed and sat beside him. She began to talk in a private little singsong voice as she explored his ears with her fingers, He listened attentively. Her parents didn't notice a thing.

Jack is worth his weight in gold.

At closing time, Kay pulled down the shades and locked the door, and turned the 'Open' sign to 'Closed.' "Man, I'm beat," she admitted. "Let's go up to my apartment and grab something to eat."

My stomach rumbled in agreement. "Okay. Let me give the dogs a spin first."

She nodded. "I'll make a salad or something simple."

She headed up the stairs that led from her office to her home, and I clipped leashes to the dogs' collars. We went out the back door, down the alley, and around a corner to a tiny park where benches and a trickling fountain provided a cool oasis under tall trees. The dogs accomplished their task with a minimum of sniffing, and I turned around to head back to OKay Antiques, nearly running into a large young man who was walking up the path behind us.

"Oh, sorry, didn't know you were there," I apologized.

He reached down to let the dogs sniff his hand. "That's all right," he said in a slow drawl.

I hurried on, eager to get back to Kay and food. I

let myself in the back door and unclipped leashes, and the three of us ran upstairs to Kay's apartment. She stood in her small kitchen, grating carrots to sprinkle on the bowls of mixed greens sitting nearby. We gave each other wan smiles.

"That looks good," I said.

"Too hot for much else," she agreed. "Who was on the phone earlier?"

I busied myself pouring tall glasses of iced tea and setting the table with flatware and a couple of cloth napkins from the sideboard. "It was that woman you called Sunday about the flea market. We talked for a few minutes, and then I called her back after the people with the little girl left."

"Joan. Good. By the way," she leaned over the counter to look at Jack, "we need to give this dog a raise. He was terrific with the kid."

Jack thumped his tail in response, and Kay went on. "Did Joan have anything interesting to say?"

"She did, actually." I went to the counter that separates the kitchen from the dining area and picked up the salads. "She said the flea market was a nightmare from beginning to end this year."

Kay perked up. "Oh, good, a disaster movie."

I laughed. "That would pack them in, wouldn't it?" I placed our salads on the table, and Kay followed me with a plate of crusty rolls and the butter dish. We sat in our accustomed places. "A flea market disaster movie. I like it."

"So would our plot involve some natural disaster? A huge sinkhole in the parking lot that swallows up a lot of cars and a senior citizen bus—"

"And our hero is forced to rappel down the side of the hole to save them, using a long orange extension cord from the donut-hole booth he'd been running," I threw in.

"Good, good. Meanwhile, terrorists are taking over the various booths and cutting prices in order to undermine our way of life." Kay took a bite of salad.

"Their ultimate goal, of course, is to conquer the used hubcap booth, because their leader is angry that the only hubcap in existence not represented is the one he needs for his car," I added. "And of course only one title fits this epic—"

Our eyes locked, and we said together, "Flee!"

Kay snorted. "Hollywood's loss is obviously Willow Falls' gain."

"I know, but I'm too tired to start a new career tonight."

"So what did Joan say, anyway?"

I broke open a roll and spread butter on it. "They started with a planning committee of ten people, and some of them moved away and one of them fell out of a tree and before long only five of them were left to do everything."

"Sounds like an Agatha Christie plot."

"I'm not sure we can work Miss Marple into our disaster epic. That's about as far as we got during the first call. So I called her back when we had that lull about an hour ago."

"I saw you dialing the phone and thought the world might be ending."

51

"Yeah, well, at least the numbers on your office phone are big enough for me to see to dial. Anyway, Joan said they muddled through the planning part, and then on Saturday it was just one thing after another. The guy who was in charge of keeping order in the parking lot was arrested for drunk driving the night before, so a bunch of teenagers directed the traffic and it got all snarled up."

"You didn't say anything about that when you got here on Saturday."

I took a bite of roll and chewed before answering. "It must have happened after I left."

"Proof once more that timing is everything. So was that it, a small committee, a DUI, and a traffic jam?"

"Nope. The day also included an elderly shopper who collapsed and had to be taken to the hospital, and because of the parking lot snafu they had trouble getting the ambulance in. Apparently he's still unconscious and the prognosis isn't very good."

She sobered. "Gosh, how awful."

"Yeah. I almost forgot to ask her about the guy selling frogs. But that turned out to be part of the general weirdness. She said that right after the ambulance took away the poor old man, a shouting match erupted at one of the booths. She went running over, and it was the guy selling the frogs and some woman screaming at each other. Or I guess it was the woman screaming."

"Hmmm, maybe they were her frogs or something. A jilted lover, and he stole her frogs and was selling them for revenge—"

"That's more far-fetched than our disaster movie plot," I said. "But something was certainly going on between them. Joan said the woman was yelling that if he didn't do something she was going to kill him, and she looked dead serious about it."

Kay shook her head. "Wow. And to think you missed all the fireworks."

"That's not all. Just as Joan was about to intervene, the woman leaned over and swept everything off the guy's table. She hit them so hard that some of them flew about ten feet, and one hit Joan on the shin and left a big bruise. And the guy took off running, and they never saw him again."

"So I guess you're not going to find him to give back that ugly frog."

"Most likely not."

"What about the woman?"

"What about her?"

"I don't know, did she gather up the fallen frogs or apologize for making a scene or anything?"

"Nope. She stomped away and that was the last they saw of her as well. Joan has no record of who the guy was. No one on her committee could remember if he'd registered for a booth ahead of time or showed up that morning and set one up. Joan said she finally picked up all the frogs and put them in her car. Actually, she asked me if I'd like to have them."

"Right, they could keep your ugly one company."

"Great. I could have several ugly frogs instead of just one. But Dan said this morning that they need some more donations for the auction. I could give him the frogs."

Kay looked dubious. "Would anyone actually bid on them? You don't want to be in the position of having to pay people to take them away. Kind of defeats the fund raising aspect of the event."

"True. But maybe we could claim they're dog toys. Dog lovers will buy anything for their pets."

6

I parked in the shade on the east side of the building and turned off the ignition. "I'll just be a minute, you guys. Be good."

Jack and Emily Ann both wagged as I got out of the car and locked the door. I couldn't help remembering a rainy night several months ago when Bob had done the same thing—left me waiting in the car while he went into this grocery store. Where he was kidnapped by a mysterious woman in a red suit. I'd only known him a few weeks at that point, but the resulting mayhem had accelerated our getting acquainted process.

A lot.

I smiled as I hurried inside, glad that the chance of my being kidnapped today was probably zero. I didn't even need to go into the store proper. My destination was the bulletin board just inside the entrance.

It had been Kay's idea to post a notice for someone to mow my grass, and she'd whipped one out on her computer after dinner. She'd even given me a small container of thumb tacks in case none were available

55

on the board. No wonder she'd been able to run her store alone as long as she had—efficiency ran through her veins.

The Food Right's bulletin board was large, with a variety of notices stuck to its cork surface. The offerings included in-home child care or pet sitting services; yoga lessons; wiretapping detection; RV rentals; inexpensive wedding flowers; tutoring on a variety of subjects; cemetery lots; recipes for fibromyalgia sufferers; Bible empowerment classes; scrapbooking groups; recovery from scrapbooking groups; and a free lizard cage.

None were from people who wanted to mow lawns.

I pinned up my half-sheet of paper and turned to go, bumping into a woman entering the store. We both took a step back to keep our balance. "Oh!" I exclaimed. "I'm so sorry, I wasn't paying attention."

The woman was Mrs. Johnson. It couldn't have been anyone else. "That's quite all right, Mrs. McGuire. I didn't realize you were here, or I would have been more careful."

Not much I could reply to that. "I was just posting a notice for someone to mow my grass. Must run, I don't want to leave the dogs in the car too long."

"No indeed, that can be dangerous. I'm in a hurry myself, I'm late for the library board meeting. Good day." She inclined her head and proceeded into the store, the skirt of her silk shirtwaist swaying with her walk. I thought I detected a couple of curly brown poodle hairs on it as she passed me.

The sun was sinking below the horizon when I turned into my driveway and wound uphill to the garage. I considered running over the lawn mower as I passed it but decided that would be petty. Besides, it might damage my car. I opened the back hatch for the dogs; they jumped to the ground. Jack shook himself and Emily Ann stretched. Then both turned alertly to look along the drive, and I realized that a buzzing noise I'd been ignoring was getting louder. The noise increased in pitch and intensity until at last a figure hurtled into sight and slid to a stop a few feet from me.

The buzz came from a very small motorcycle, which mercifully was switched off immediately. The rider looked far too large for his vehicle; I glanced beyond him to see if perhaps a troupe of Shriners was practicing for a parade and had chosen my place to do so. But evidently the hulk on the bike was alone.

When he climbed off his vehicle I saw he was over six feet tall, with a thick column for a body. A too-small half helmet perched atop heavy blond hair that fell over his forehead. The face was young, at most mid-twenties, clean-shaven, with wide, guileless blue eyes. One of the voices in my head said dryly, "Just what you needed, the original beardless youth."

"Can I help you?" I said. Perhaps he was lost.

He swept off the helmet. "I was hoping I could help you." His slow drawl struck me as somehow odd, but I couldn't think why. "Did you pin up this notice at the shop?"

He held out a piece of white paper, which I had no

trouble recognizing as the half sheet I had put up at the Food Right.

"I certainly did. Why did you take it down? How are people supposed to see it and call me?" I couldn't help a note of exasperation in my voice. I could almost hear the grass growing as we stood talking.

"But they won't need to. I mean, I can do it. I followed you from the shop, you see."

I did see, and I didn't like it. Women as a rule do not care to be followed to their homes by large young men whom they do not know. Of course, I did have two very protective dogs. I glanced down at Jack and Emily Ann, and discovered they were no longer beside me. Jack was wagging his way over to the stranger, and Emily Ann had gone to a spot of too-tall grass and settled down to watch.

"You followed me? You can't do that. I think you'd better be on your way." I did my best to appear commanding.

He bent over to let Jack sniff his hand. Jack wagged harder. "But don't you need someone to mow your grass?"

Damn. He had me there. "Do you have experience?"

"Oh, yes, ma'am," he drawled, standing upright again to tower over me. "I can mow any grass, anywhere."

"Do you have your own equipment?" As soon as I said it, I could picture Kay cracking up and waggling her eyebrow at me. I felt a blush begin, which I hoped could be passed off as the reflection of the setting sun.

He looked startled. "You mean, like my own lawn mower?" I nodded. "Couldn't I just use that one?" He pointed.

I knew I should have put it away this morning. "Well, yes, I suppose you could."

He took this for acceptance, and a huge smile split his face. "Great! Shall I begin now?"

"That's not—" I began, and stopped. Why not give him a try? No telling if anyone else would even reply to my ad, especially since it was no longer on the notice board at the Food Right but instead had followed me home like a lost kitten. "Oh, all right. But not tonight, it will be dark soon. Come back tomorrow a little after six. Six in the evening, I mean." Most guys his age were probably not aware that there was also a six in the morning, but I didn't want to take any chances. I could imagine this one coming back before dawn.

"Great! I'll see you tomorrow then." He looked so pleased that I felt guilty about my suspicions over being followed.

"Tomorrow," I agreed, then asked. "What's your name?"

"H—Hank," he said. "Call me Hank."

The next morning I let myself in the back door of OKay Antiques. Kay looked up from where she sat at her desk.

"Guess what!" We said it simultaneously, then laughed at each other.

"You first," she said. I sat in the chair beside her desk.

"Your ad worked," I said. "A guy is going to mow my grass this afternoon."

Kay nodded. "That's great."

"And I saw Mrs. Johnson at the Food Right. Did you know she's on the library board?"

"Yes, they appointed her about a month ago. I hope she doesn't hang around the library much. She'd scare the customers away."

An unbidden image of Mrs. Johnson at storytime propelled itself into my mind. "She scares me," I admitted. "So what's your news?"

She bounced a little on her chair. "I may have found a new employee."

In spite of the fact that I wanted to work fewer hours, I felt a pang at her eagerness. "Yeah? Who?"

"Haven't met her yet, we just talked on the phone last night. She talks like she really knows antiques."

"What's her name? Is she from around here?" I didn't think she could be a native or Kay would already know her.

"Rebecca Bleck," she said, enunciating carefully, "and no, she's from Chicago. She said she's thinking about moving here permanently and wants to try Willow Falls for a few months. She's coming in later this morning."

"For an interview, you mean?"

Kay shook her head. "We did that on the phone. I said I'd try her. I figure if she's as persuasive with customers as she was with me she'll sell a lot of antiques."

"But Kay, what if we don't like her when we meet

her? What if she robs you? What if—"

"What if you stop being the human resources manager? You left that line of work, remember?" Kay thrust her chair back and stood up. "I'm not stupid, Louisa. I can fire her if she doesn't work out, and meanwhile you get your life back, which I thought you wanted."

I looked up at her from where I still sat. "Just part of it," I said. "And I'm not too sure which part."

7

"Good morning. Kay Chelton?" The woman who entered the store shortly after we opened brushed a strand of dark hair with a few hints of gray behind her ear with perfectly manicured fingertips. Some very large diamonds winked at me from her rings.

"No, I'm Louisa McGuire. Let me get Kay for you." The woman's clothes and grooming indicated she could afford to buy most of the store, and I'd be happy to let Kay sell it to her.

"Oh, you're Louisa," the woman smiled. A trick of the light across her glasses kept me from seeing her eyes. "I'm Rebecca Bleck. Your cousin told me all about you."

Ah. The new employee. "How nice to meet you. I'll fetch Kay."

I left her scanning the stock. Kay was at her desk in the back. "Rebecca Bleck is here," I said.

Kay jumped up. "Great. What's she like?"

"Rich."

This got a laugh. "Good, maybe she won't need the pittance I can pay her and will work for the fun of it."

She headed out to the front of the store and greeted Rebecca. I remained where I was to listen.

"I absolutely love this Victorian dovecote over here," Rebecca said, "and these Delft Biblical tiles are wonderful. Your stock is really first class."

"Thank you," Kay said. Their voices moved away. "Take a look at this Frank Furness desk. It came from a banker's estate in St. Louis."

They spoke the same language. Rebecca knew her stuff and would probably work out fine. Kay wouldn't need me in the store now, and I could go to California with a clear conscience.

If I wanted to go to California.

The bell over the front door jangled, and I hurried out. But it wasn't a customer, it was Ed, imposing in his police chief's uniform.

"Hey, Louisa," he said. At the sound of his voice Jack, who had been curled on his cushion behind the counter, unfolded and hurried over to greet him. Ed leaned down to scratch behind Jack's ears. "Did you guys have a good run this morning at the dog park?"

"They did indeed," I said. "Emily Ann's flaked out on that sofa. Your mother's new dog tried to run circles around her and she had to uphold her reputation as the fastest dog in Willow Falls."

He laughed. "That Prince is a piece of work, isn't he? I couldn't believe it when my mother came home with a dog. Thank god for the dog park. The mutt would be climbing the walls and swinging from the chandeliers without it."

"You didn't know your mother was planning to get

a dog?" I asked.

He shook his head. "I'm not sure how much planning went into it. She never said a word ahead of time about wanting a dog, just came home with it on Saturday."

"Where did she get him? Was Prince Henri a rescue dog?"

"She didn't say. For all I know she got him at that flea market in High Cross. That's where I thought she was going that morning."

"She was there, I ran into her," I said, "but I never saw anything as cute as Prince Henri for sale." I looked past Ed and saw Kay and Rebecca returning from their tour of the store's stock. "Ed, let me introduce Kay's new assistant, Rebecca Bleck. Rebecca, this is Ed Johnson, our chief of police and a good friend."

Ed gave me a startled look at the word "assistant," but quickly put on a smile as he turned. "Good morning." He reached out to shake hands.

Rebecca gave him her hand briefly, then said, "That's surely not a police dog, is it?" She looked at Jack, who sat on Ed's foot. She did not seem impressed with Jack.

Ed laughed. "I'd love to have him on the force. We could make him our press officer. No, Jack is one of Louisa's personal bodyguards." He turned his attention to Kay. "I just wanted to stop by and say thanks again, hon, for the gift." He reached for her shoulders and kissed her on the cheek. As he released her he said, "I took it home last night, and my mother absolutely loathes it. I put it on the mantle, and she glared at it all evening."

"Ed, she already doesn't like me, it won't help for you to tease her like that," Kay scolded. "It's for your desk at work." She was trying not to grin.

"Hey, it's my house," he protested. "I can have a frog on the mantle if I want to."

"Watch it, buster, or she'll move back to her own place and no one will be around to take care of you. I'm not going to do your laundry, that's for sure." To Rebecca she said, "Ed's mother keeps house for him and his daughter."

Rebecca ignored this aside. "Frog?" She raised an eyebrow.

The bell jangled again and two ladies walked in, their eyes already scanning the room for treasures. Kay turned towards them but Rebecca said, "Oh, let me," and soon she was in laughing conversation with the pair. Before long she led them to a display of vintage hankies. Kay looked on approvingly.

"Who is she, anyway?" Ed asked in a low voice. Kay turned back to him.

"My new employee," she said. "It's just too darned busy for me and Louisa, so I'm giving her a trial."

"Yeah, but who is she? Where did she come from?"

Exactly what I wanted to know. Ed and I looked at Kay expectantly. She glared back.

"I'll tell you later," she said. "She's right there, I can't talk about her now."

"Meet us for dinner at the Bluebird," I told Ed.

"It's a date."

Kay raised a bland eyebrow at me. "Aren't you

forgetting something?" I looked at her blankly. She went on, "Don't you have a hot date with a yard guy?"

I groaned. "I forgot. I have to go right home. This guy is coming to mow my grass tonight," I explained to Ed.

He looked amused. "Why Louisa, I'm surprised at you. Bob is hardly out of sight and you're seeing another man."

I was starting to wish I'd never met Bob, so I wouldn't have to put up with this teasing. Or maybe I should wish my lawn away. "Oh yeah, I'm so attracted to guys thirty years younger than me who talk like—" I suddenly realized what Hank's voice had reminded me of. "—like bad John Wayne imitations."

Rebecca led her two customers up to the counter then, near where we were standing. She slid her eyes sideways at me. Great, she probably thought I meant what I'd just said about young guys. Kay turned to show her how to ring up the sale, and Rebecca carefully wrapped a Noritake teacup and saucer in paper. Before she put them in a bag she reached into her pocket and drew out a cluster of small silk roses, which she taped to the package. It looked charming.

"There," she cooed to the ladies. "You're my first customers here, and I brought these along for whoever that turned out to be."

They were delighted, and Kay looked like she had just found the Holy Grail. I discovered my teeth were grinding together, and I made my jaw relax into something resembling a smile.

8

I arrived home earlier that afternoon than I'd expected. The last hour had been light on customers and Kay didn't need me with Rebecca there. I gathered up the dogs and sped home, glancing at the sky as I drove. The wind was herding dark clouds across the horizon. If it were going to rain I hoped it would do it later, after the mowing was accomplished.

I figured I could change clothes and grab a snack before Hank arrived. But his little motorcycle already sat beside my garage when I got home. There was no sign of him, but since I'm always early for appointments myself I could only approve.

The garage door rose smoothly in response to the remote control, and I parked my car next to Bob's. I made a mental note to drive his tomorrow, to keep its tires limber, or whatever happens when you let a car sit for too long. I let the dogs out of the car and paused by the bike. Unless it had arrived alone, Hank must be somewhere around the place. "Hello?" I called out. "Hank?"

No answer, but both dogs lifted their heads, then charged around the house to the left. I followed them, and called again, "Hank? Where are you?"

The dogs were out of sight. I heard Jack bark once, then some rustling noises. I picked up my pace. As I rounded the corner I nearly ran into Hank, who was charging full speed from the opposite direction.

"Oh!" he exclaimed, sidestepping to miss me. "Hello!"

I looked up at his pink face. He must have spent the day in the sun, and his fair skin was set off by the white oxford cloth shirt he wore. He looked awfully immaculate for doing yard work. "Hi. What are you doing?"

"I was looking around to see how much yard you have. So I'd know about how long it will take to mow. You know. I got here early because my other mowing job cancelled on me." He gave me a wide smile, shoving his hands into the pockets of his dark slacks.

"That's too bad. Who else do you mow for?"

The smile faltered. "Um, the Browns. Over on the other side of town."

I shook my head. "Don't know them, though my cousin probably does. Listen, I need to change clothes. Let me get you the key to the shed so you can get started."

"Great!" The smile came back.

I led him around to the front door and unlocked it. He followed me into the entry way. "Hang on, let me put my purse away and I'll get the key." I left him looking around at the boxes I had not yet unpacked from moving in a month ago.

The thing is, my house is unusual. It's octagonal, so none of the rooms are the usual rectangle. A circular stairway leads up to a large space with walls of floor-to-ceiling glass, undivided except for a wedge on the north side for a bedroom and bath. I'd unpacked the basics, but I was still struggling to figure out where everything should go.

I trotted up the stairs to the main part of the house and dropped my bag in a chair. The shed key hung on a hook inside the cabinet under the sink. I grabbed it and went back down. Hank was kneeling and petting both dogs, who looked blissful.

"These are great dogs," he said.

I beamed at him. I'm a sucker for anyone who likes Emily Ann and Jack. "They are, aren't they? Jack is only visiting for a few weeks, though. Emily Ann will really miss him when we have to send him to California." Emily Ann was not the only one who would miss Jack.

Hank stood, and Jack sat on one of his loafered feet. "California?"

"Yes, that's where his owner is...I mean, just moved to...there...California. Berkeley actually." My voice alerted Jack. He left Hank and came to me, looking worried. I decided I'd better change the subject or I'd start sobbing in front of this poor guy who only wanted to make a few bucks mowing my grass. "Okay, here's the key to the shed by the garage. The mower is still sitting outside, but you'll need to get into the shed for the trimmer thingy for doing the edges and around the trees. I'll let you get started. Let me know if you need anything else."

He took the key. "Thank you, ma'am. I'll get on it," he drawled in that John Wayne voice. Both dogs followed him outside.

I closed the door after them and went back upstairs. Straight to the kitchen. I found a few crackers that had not yet gone stale. Some sliced provolone cheese that was beginning to stiffen lingered in the fridge. I had been too distracted by the thought of Bob leaving to remember to buy food. I stacked a few crackers on a plate, bent a couple of cheese slices back and forth until they broke into quarter circles, and carried it all to the bedroom.

A stack of boxes in the corner made a handy place for the plate. Munching, I pulled a pair of loose cotton pants out of the closet, and found a soft old tee shirt in a drawer. The clothes I'd worn to work went into a basket on the closet floor. I stepped into the adjoining bathroom and washed my face in cold water, then rinsed and dried my glasses. I now felt ready to face whatever the rest of the day might hold. Back in the bedroom I picked up the plate once more, and paused to frown at the box it had been resting on.

Those boxes, which had waited patiently for weeks to be unpacked, were taunting me. Should I unpack them, and stay in Willow Falls? Should I leave them packed and go to California? Maybe I should just chuck them unopened. I'd gotten by without their contents for several weeks. In fact some had been packed up since I left Seattle, after my husband and parents

70

died. I even had the last odds and ends from my parents' papers. There were memories in those boxes I'd rather not stir up. I felt stuck, unable to make a decision about anything. I bared my teeth and tried a low growl. The boxes were not visibly cowed.

It occurred to me that I had not yet heard the growl of the mower, or even the whine of the trimmer. I carried the plate of cheese and crackers over to the window and looked out. Hank was standing near the shed with hands on hips, flanked by the dogs, looking down at the lawn mower. His shoulders slumped.

I knew just how he felt.

My first instinct was to run down and see if I could help. The voice in my head that jeers said, "Help how? You don't know how to start the darned thing. That's why you put up the notice at the Food Right." And the voice that worries about everyone's feelings said, "He'll be hurt if you act like he's incompetent." The impatient voice butted in, "Leave him alone. You're paying him to mow. If he doesn't mow, don't pay him." I bit into a cracker, hoping the crunching would drown all the voices.

I waited a bit before going outside. When I did, Hank was kneeling beside the mower, peering at it closely.

"I couldn't get it started either," I told him.

He looked over his shoulder at me. "Maybe it's possessed," he ventured.

I considered this. "Maybe, but it would have to be possessed by an awfully lazy demon. I'd be more inclined to the possession theory if it started careening all over and we couldn't get it to turn off."

He nodded seriously. "Good point." Rising to his feet he added, "Perhaps it's dead, and there is no after-life."

"If it's dead, I don't care about its afterlife, I care whether it's still under warranty." I glared at the silent mower.

Hank laughed. He started to speak again, but whatever he was going to say was lost in a flash of lightening and clap of thunder so close I felt my hair lift. Ominous clouds scudded overhead, and just as suddenly as the thunder they let go of their load. Before we could move we were soaked.

"Let's get this stuff inside!" I grabbed the trimmer, which was leaning against a tree, and lugged it to the shed. Hank followed with the mower. At least its wheels worked. "Come on, let's lock up here and go dry off. You can't ride a motorcycle in this rain."

"Oh, but—I'll be all right. A little rain won't hurt me."

"No, come on, it will probably let up in a bit. I don't want to imagine you being hit by lightning," I said.

"Well...okay. Thanks!"

We hurried to the house. Another crack of thunder encouraged us to run. The four of us burst through the front door, laughing and dripping. I left Hank and the dogs in the entry while I fetched towels to dry us all off. When I returned, he was looking at a box of DVDs I'd opened but not unpacked.

"You've got *High Anxiety*," he remarked. "I loved

that."

I handed him a towel, which he applied to his face and hair. "Me too," I said. "But I can't watch it very often because I get that song stuck in my head. Emily Ann, let me dry you off."

She came to lean on me while I ran the towel over her sleek body.

"Can I help?" Hank asked.

"Sure, you can do Jack," I said, tossing him another towel. He patted his knee and Jack obligingly went to him. Soon both dogs were passably dry, and Hank and I were no longer dripping.

"You certainly have violent storms," Hank commented, as another flash of lightening was followed almost immediately by the boom of thunder.

"This isn't much, just your garden variety summer storm. You must not be from around here."

"No, I—I grew up further east." His eye fell again on the box of videos. "Goodness, *Time Bandits*! I saw that just once, when I was about nine, and thought it was amazing. I dreamed about it for a week."

"Want to watch it?" The invitation was out before I thought. "We could rustle up something to eat and ride out the storm."

"Oh, but I'd be imposing." His tone was hopeful.

"You'll be doing me a favor. I'll be able to ignore these boxes for a few more hours without feeling guilty. And it can't be safe to ride that little bike in a storm. Come on upstairs and let's see about some food. Grab that disk, would you?" That was when I remembered the state of my larder. I was Mother Hubbard's first cousin and Hank looked like he could eat a mountain of food.

"This is such an interesting house," he commented as he emerged at the top of the circular stairs. "I've never seen anything like it."

"Thanks. I really like it, I just can't seem to figure out where everything should go. Plus we've been really busy at my cousin's antique shop. I'm starting to think I'll never get unpacked."

"Perhaps you could float some of the bookcases out from the wall, or turn them perpendicular. You could make a reading nook."

He wasn't good with the mower, but had real possibilities as an interior designer. "That might be fun. I'll have to experiment. Have a seat. Wine okay? I hope you like pizza. A place down the hill delivers, I'll call them."

"Mmm, lovely," he said, looking around for a chair.

The word fell oddly on my ear. Lovely. I'd known a fair number of young men Hank's age when I'd been the human resources manager for Notel Software. They'd ranged from software engineers to salesmen to accountants, geeks to sleek sophisticates, and I couldn't imagine one of them responding to the suggestion of pizza with "lovely."

I gave a mental shrug. Maybe it was an east coast thing, or he'd been brought up by an English mother or something. I picked up the phone. "Veggie okay?" Hank nodded enthusiastically. He'd taken a seat on the sofa, and now had a dog snuggled against each side. "Hello, Mario?" I said when the phone was answered. "This is Louisa McGuire. Yes, good, how about you? Yeah, it's pouring. Oh, she's fine, I'll tell her you asked about her. Can you stand to make a delivery? Twenty minutes? Wonderful. Yes, the veggie, but make it a large. Right. Exactly. Thanks." I glanced at Hank once more. "Hang on, Mario, I think you'd better make that two."

9

The next morning was still dripping and blustering when I let myself into the store. I hung up the umbrella I hadn't bothered to open for the few steps from the car to the door. Then I grabbed the towel I keep on a hook by the back door and gave the dogs a quick wipe; their rainwater rinse left their fur soft and shiny. When they were done I remembered to dab at my own hair before crossing the crowded room and emerging into the lighted store.

Kay was at the sales counter, opening mail. "Junk, junk, more junk," I heard her mutter as the dogs rushed to her side. "Emily Ann! Jack! It's you!"

She reached into a pocket and brought out a couple of small treats. Both dogs immediately sat, identical angelic expressions on their faces. Kay's lips twitched in amusement as she handed each a morsel. "Okay," she said, releasing them from the sit. "You guys settle in for the day. Looks like a good one for a snooze."

Emily Ann lives to nap. She headed for her current favorite sofa, climbed up and turned around twice before folding her long legs. She closed her eyes with a sigh. Jack strolled off to check the perimeters of the store.

Kay held out a dog biscuit to me. "Hungry?"

"Mmmm, yum. I suppose I'd have to sit on the floor in front of you first?"

"Of course. You know you have to work for your treats."

I shook my head. "In that case I'll pass. If I sat on the floor it would take far more than the energy in a dog biscuit to get me back up again."

"Don't tell me you stayed up late." Kay raised an eyebrow. She's familiar with my early to bed, early to rise proclivities.

I shook my head. "Not really. It's just the way the floor gets farther away every year. Haven't you noticed?"

"I have indeed." She glanced at her watch. "Time to open. Would you do the honors?"

"You bet." I walked across the store to the front door, where I pulled up the shades and flipped the lock. "Ed's mother was back at the dog park this morning," I said as I turned over the "Closed" sign to "Open."

She was again immersed in the mail. "Was she? That's nice."

"I think something's really odd there," I continued. No response. "What are you reading?"

She finally looked up. "What?"

"What are you reading? I'm talking about Mrs. Johnson and you're not reacting."

She brandished a sheet of paper covered with dense type. "Announcement from that auctioneer up in Iowa. He's got a farm sale coming up, might be worth going to." Kay lives for a good country auction. "So what did you say about Mrs. Johnson?"

"That she was back at the dog park this morning with Prince Henri, and something odd is going on."

"You know how I feel about small yappy dogs, not to mention Mrs. Johnson. Seems like a perfectly natural pairing to me. Though Ed said he thought the poodle was simply ridiculous at first, but he's beginning to grow on him."

"Yeah, but where did she get him? Most people will tell you everything about it, but she doesn't say a word."

"That's what she's like. Maybe she just found him."

"Only a total moron would lose something that valuable," I stated with conviction.

"You think he's valuable?"

"I do, actually. It worries me."

Kay waved a hand. "I don't think you need to be concerned. You know Ed, if anything is wrong he'll find it."

"That's what worries me. If she had to give him up I'm not sure what she'd do. I may ask around—" I broke off at a crash from the back room. Jack came running, barking his deep Basset-y bark. He never barks in the store, having figured out from the first that all kinds of people are allowed. He scrambled past us and through the door into the back room.

"Oh!" exclaimed a woman's voice. "Get away!"

I hurried after Jack, Kay behind me. Rebecca was standing against the stairway. As I came through the door I saw Jack startle away from her. I dropped to my knees and said sharply, "Jack, here!"

He stopped barking and wheeled around, throwing himself against me. I put a hand on his back and murmured, "You're okay now. Stay with me."

Kay hurried over to Rebecca. "Are you all right?"

Rebecca took a couple of steps away from the stairs and patted at her clothing. "I'm fine. The dear little doggie just startled me, is all. I'm afraid he made me drop that figurine." She pointed to some shards of china a few feet from the door into the store.

Kay and Rebecca turned to look at Jack, leaning against me. Rebecca's eyes rose to meet mine, and an expression of pure hatred flashed over her face. I flinched. The glare was replaced so quickly by a smile that I wondered if I had actually seen it. Oh yeah, said a wary voice in my head, you saw that.

"Jack, what is wrong with you?" Kay asked, looking perplexed.

What's wrong with *her*, said the indignant voice in my head. I ran a hand down Jack's back. Tension stiffened his fur. "He's not used to someone else coming in the back door," I said. Kay's face cleared.

"Of course," she said. She turned to Rebecca. "Jack is very protective of Louisa, but he wouldn't hurt a fly."

Rebecca nodded, smoothed down her linen jacket once more, and said, "I think I heard the door. Shall I go check on the customers?"

"You bet. And I'll get the mail out of the way." Kay followed Rebecca. Jack and I remained where we were. Both our hearts were beating fast.

"Did she try to kick you?" I murmured to him, rubbing his ears. "You'd better stay away from her, sweet Jack. Maybe you wouldn't hurt a fly, but I bet *she* would without thinking twice."

In spite of the rain we had a steady supply of customers all morning. I sold a beaded reticule to a collector from Georgia, a framed baby kimono to a woman whose son had just become a father, and a dollhouse family carved of poplar that would now live in a Victorian mansion just their size. At a little past one I realized I was starving.

"Kay, I'm going to the Bluebird for some lunch," I told her. "Want me to bring you something?"

I had forgotten Rebecca, who had hearing that a bat would envy. She said from behind me, "Go with her, Kay. I'll be fine here by myself."

"No, you two go," said Kay. "You can bring me back a sandwich."

After that look she'd given me earlier, I did not want to sit across a table from Rebecca and be polite over food. My appetite disappeared at the thought.

Rebecca walked around me to the counter. "No, no, I insist. Now that you have an assistant you should make use of me."

An assistant? What the heck have I been for the past year? the indignant voice in my head piped up.

Okay, part of the time I'd been a total basket case—but Rebecca didn't know that. The paranoid voice chimed in with, Maybe Kay told her. The loyal voice said no, Kay would never do that.

"I brought my lunch," Rebecca went on, "so you two go along and have a good time. I'll pop into the back for a bite when no customers need me."

"Wellll," Kay said slowly, looking back and forth between us.

"Go on, I'll be fine. If anything comes up I can't handle, I'll call the café, how's that?"

"If you're sure."

"I'm sure. Now scoot."

Kay grabbed a couple of umbrellas from the back. I had a private word with each dog, telling them to be good and watch out for Rebecca. Then Kay and I closed the front door behind us and dodged the puddles between OKay Antiques and the Bluebird Cafe.

The cafe was packed, but I spotted a table. Our favorite booth was occupied by a quartet of African American women arguing cheerfully about something. We made our way to the vacant table, hung our umbrellas from the back of a chair, and sat. Kay peered around me to study the daily specials on the chalkboard.

"Oh good," she said, "Dorothy's made her spring stew."

"Is that the one with asparagus and peas?"

"And fennel. Yeah. I wonder if she made the caraway seed bread to go with it."

"She surely did," said Cleta, walking up with tinkling glasses of iced tea. "Did you girls close the shop or leave the dogs in charge?"

Kay grinned. "The dogs are in charge, but my new assistant Rebecca is helping them make change."

Cleta nodded. "Oh yes, the one from Chicago. How is she working out?"

"She's great," Kay said enthusiastically. "She knows a lot and she's wonderful with customers."

I bit my bottom lip. I was afraid I might say something about how wonderful Rebecca was when she wasn't trying to kick my dog. I met Cleta's eyes. She looked at me steadily, then gave a little nod. "What will you have for lunch, then?" she asked. "Kay, I know you want the stew. You always like that one. Louisa?"

"Sounds good to me too."

"You bet. Won't be long."

Cleta hurried off to the kitchen, and Kay leaned back in her chair with a sigh. "It's nice being able to have lunch together," she said. "I hadn't noticed I was hungry."

"And now you get to have Dorothy's spring stew."

"Life is good," she pronounced solemnly. We looked at each other and laughed.

A stir in the corner booth caught my eye as the four women gathered up their purses and left, still arguing amiably. I was about to suggest to Kay that we switch tables when another trio standing by the door spotted the empty table and headed toward it. The curly headed woman leading them stopped when she reached us.

"Hi Kay, hi Louisa," she said. It was Eileen, who owns Trellis Island, the garden art store around the corner from Kay's shop. "Did you all close the store or leave the dogs in charge?"

"Oh, the dogs are in charge," Kay replied. "They always have been."

Eileen laughed and led her party on to the back booth. Kay said to me, "Did the lawn guy show up last night and mow?"

"He showed up," I said, "but it started raining before he was able to mow." I decided not to mention Hank's inability to start my lawnmower; I knew what Kay would have to say about that.

"Too bad. Now your grass will grow more than ever. Who is he, anyway?"

"His name is Hank."

"Hank what?"

I didn't think he'd said his last name. "I can't remember."

She shook her head. "Sometimes I think you're losing your mind."

"Me too. It's probably a combination of age and moving. Every time I need something at home, I have to stop and think if I've unpacked it and where it is. The only place I can rely on autopilot is at your place. Maybe I should just move in with you until all those boxes get unpacked."

"Nuh uh, if you moved in with me you'd never unpack. You need help, that's all. Want me to round up some high school kids to work on it? You could ply them with pizzas and your boxes would be empty in no time."

I wasn't sure I could afford pizza for more than one young person. I thought about the way Hank had casually demolished one large pizza by himself last night, then absorbed two thirds of the second one. But Kay's words did stir something in my brain.

"Earth to Louisa," I heard Kay say. "Come back, Cleta's here with food."

"Sorry, didn't mean to space out."

Cleta set her tray on the table and gave me a kindly pat on the shoulder. "This will fix you right up," she said, placing steaming bowls of fragrant stew in front of us. A plate heaped with slices of bread followed. "Enjoy." She took her tray and hurried off to the next task.

"So how about those high school kids to help you unpack?" Kay asked. She picked up her spoon and sipped some broth from her bowl. "Mmmm, this is so good."

I took a bite, then reached for some bread. "Thanks, but probably not. The problem is this house is so different that I'm having trouble deciding where to put things. And I feel like if I don't do it myself I'll never know where anything is. But maybe Hank could help me. He's tall and strong and could probably use the money."

Kay frowned. "Hank? Oh, the yard guy. Do you know him well enough to have him working in the house?"

Before I could say something about whether she knew Rebecca well enough to leave the store in her hands when she'd only interviewed her over the phone, a deep voice interrupted our conversation. "Good afternoon, ladies." It was Ed. He pulled out one of the empty chairs at our table and sat down. "Did you close the store, or leave the dogs in charge?"

"You're forgetting I have a new assistant," Kay said. "Rebecca said she could handle it, so I thought I'd give her the chance."

Ed nodded. "Oh, yes, Rebecca. Say, did you hear about the excitement at my house this morning?"

We shook our heads.

Cleta hurried up to the table and set a steaming mug of coffee in front of Ed. "The usual?" she asked. He nodded. Off she went. He spooned a liberal amount of sugar into the dark brew and stirred, then took a sip.

Kay waited until the mug was back on the table, then said, "So what happened at your house?"

"Somebody broke in," he said.

"What!" Kay laughed. "Who would break into the police chief's house?"

"Probably some crazy person. I'd already left for work, and Mother had taken her Prince to the dog park. Faith had just gotten up and was getting dressed for school and heard a noise downstairs. She thought it was her grandmother, back early from the park. She says she called out something like 'Nanna, is that you?' The noises stopped, then there was a crash, then footsteps from the kitchen. She got scared and went into her room and locked the door and called me."

85

"Smart kid," Kay said.

Ed beamed. "Yeah, she takes after her mother. Anyway, I hurried home and found the back door standing open and the window over the kitchen sink smashed."

"Is that how they got in?" Kay asked. "By breaking the window?"

"No, that's the weird thing. It was broken from the inside. The burglar threw the sugar bowl through the window, then left. How weird is that?"

We digested that. Then I said, "Sounds like temper to me." They both looked at me. "Well, it reminds me of how Roger would act if he didn't get his way. He'd stamp around the house and pick up something breakable, preferably something of mine, and smash it on the floor. Then he'd storm out and leave the mess for me to clean up."

Kay looked shocked. "You never told me this before."

I shrugged. I'd never told her about a lot of things Roger did. "You couldn't do anything," I said. "It doesn't matter."

They were both silent for a moment, then Ed said, "You may be right. Whoever broke in must have thought the house was empty and was furious that Faith was home. I'm just glad the only victims were a window and a sugar bowl."

Cleta returned with a plate holding an enormous sandwich and a heap of fries. She plunked it down in front of Ed and pulled a ketchup bottle out of her apron pocket. "Is Faith all right?" she asked. "That must have been scary when she heard your burglar downstairs this morning."

We all take for granted that Cleta knows everything. Ed assured her, "She's fine, rearing to find out who it was. I just can't imagine why anyone would break into my house."

"Your mother does have some awfully nice things," Cleta pointed out.

"Yeah, like that exquisite frog Louisa found for you," Kay said. "I bet whoever it was planned to make a bee line for the mantel and steal it."

We all laughed, and fell to eating our lunches.

10

The rain stopped while we were in the Bluebird, and we emerged after lunch to watery sunshine and thick, humid air. Ed walked the short distance to OKay Antiques with us, gave Kay a cheerful kiss, and headed off to the police station. Kay and I stood aside to let two men leave her store, then entered.

"I don't care what you say," I iterated to Kay in response to her last remark as she closed the door behind us, "whoever broke into Ed's house was either crazy, totally stupid, or did it by mistake."

"Okay, okay, you're probably right," she replied, handing me her purse to put in back. Rebecca looked up from the sales counter where she was wrapping a package for a customer. Three or four other browsers inspected our wares. Kay strolled off to answer questions and encourage sales. I headed for the back room with our purses and the umbrellas, detouring by Emily Ann's sofa to give her a pat.

She wasn't there.

Maybe someone had been interested in this sofa

and she'd moved to another so they could sit down. I gave a quick glance around and didn't see her. Then I looked to Jack's cushion by the sales counter. It was as bare as the sofa.

A jab of alarm made my neck tighten.

"Where are the dogs?" It came out louder than I expected. Everyone in the store stared at me. Rebecca frowned and continued her wrapping.

I walked the few steps to the sales counter and said again, "Where are my dogs?"

She ignored me while she slipped the wrapped item into a bag, but spots of bright pink appeared on her cheeks. "Here you go," she said, handing the bag to her customer, a young woman in a revealing tank top and torn jeans. "Thank you so much." She gave a twinkling smile that left her face the instant the girl turned to go. She looked at me and the expression in her eyes would have taken the varnish off a sailboat.

"Yes, Louisa? Did you need something?" She could easily get voice-over work, doing evil snaky creatures in scary kids' movies.

"Where are Jack and Emily Ann?" I am normally alarmed by evil snaky creatures but not when my dogs are involved.

"I had a customer," she said, opting for martyred patience, "who was allergic to dogs. I put them in the back room. I was about to let them out again. Honestly." To this last she added a little sniff.

I wanted to smack her, but my hands were full of umbrellas and purses. I moved around the sales desk to get to the back room. My hand was reaching for the

89

door knob when Rebecca went on, "Besides, it is quite inappropriate to have them here. I don't understand how Kay can allow it."

"Kay allows it," I said, "because she loves the dogs, and it is good business. Those dogs have sold more antiques than you ever will. People come from miles around to see them, they have fans all over the place. They set this store apart from all the other antique stores in Willow Falls. Furthermore—"

Kay appeared at my side and put her hand on my arm. "It's okay," she said gently, "go check on them." She reached past me, turned the knob, and pushed open the door. Then she gave me a little conspiratorial wink before she turned to Rebecca. As I stepped into the back room I heard her say, "All quite true, you'd be amazed at what a draw those two are. I started a webpage for them a while back and it got so much traffic it crashed the server."

"Yes, but—"

"And Jack is magical at keeping little kids away from china. But if someone was making a fuss about being allergic you did the right thing. Did this allergy sufferer buy anything?"

I stopped listening. "Jack? Emily Ann?" I called. I felt another stab of alarm when they did not come running. In fact it was odd that they hadn't been standing by the door to greet me when I came in. "Dogs, here!" I called again. I dropped the things in my hands on Kay's desk and looked around.

And saw that the back door to the alley was standing open.

I rushed over and looked out. No sign of the two dogs. They could have been gone nearly an hour if that woman had banished them as soon as we left for lunch. I dithered about which direction to turn, then went to the right, thinking maybe they'd gone to the little park where I sometimes walked them. I ran up the alley and across the street, nearly getting hit by a pickup truck that came fast around the corner. I ignored the shout from the driver and ran on, looking about wildly for the dogs.

"Jack! Emily Ann!" I called. I ran into the pocket park, past several people relaxing on benches. "Emily Ann, here!" I was too breathless from running and anxiety for my voice to carry far. I stopped and peered around, willing the dogs to appear from under the bushes. They didn't. I wanted to wail but didn't have enough breath left for it.

Then I heard my name being called. "Mrs. McGuire! Louisa!" I spun around and saw Hank about half a block away. With him were Emily Ann and Jack; he was holding lengths of string attached to their collars. He let go and they dashed toward me. I dropped to my knees, ignoring the mud I landed in, and opened my arms to be engulfed by wiggling dogs.

"Sweeties! What are you doing out here? You know better than to go off by yourselves," I scolded happily, hugging them. "You could have been run over. You know we have a rule about that."

Hank's feet arrived beside them and I looked up. It was a long way to his face. "Thank you. Where did you find them?"

91

He reached a hand down to help me to my feet. "About four blocks away, by the library. Got the librarian to give me the string for leashes, I wasn't sure how car-savvy they are."

"Good thinking," I said. I leaned over to brush off my knees but only succeeded in smearing mud on my hands. I shrugged and wiped them off on my butt. "Thanks so much for rescuing them."

"Any time," he drawled. I half expected him to add "little lady" but he refrained. "Do you think it will be dry enough to try again to mow your grass this evening?"

"Probably," I said. "It doesn't take long when the sun comes out. But I was wondering if you might be interested in working a few days, helping me unpack. Or do you only do yard work?"

He beamed. "That would be great. When do you want to start?"

I thought for a moment. I needed to lay in some food if Hank was going to be around. "Meet me at the house about six thirty," I told him. He nodded, gave me a quick salute, and turned to walk back the way he'd come. Jack took a step to follow.

"Here, Jack," I said, gathering up the strings tied to their collars. "We have a word or two to say to Rebecca."

I walked them around to Maple Street and led them in the front door of OKay Antiques. Kay was still talking to Rebecca by the counter. They both looked surprised to see us.

"Louisa!" Kay exclaimed. "What are you doing?

92

How did you get so muddy?"

I didn't answer, but led the two dogs up to the counter. "Did you leave that back door open on purpose?" I growled at Rebecca. "It wasn't enough to shove the dogs in the back room, you wanted them to get run over?"

Rebecca said, "What are you talking about?"

"You know exactly what I'm talking about." I held her eyes with mine. If we were dogs we'd have been in a snarling dogfight by now, each of us trying to pin the other to the floor.

Kay said, "Louisa, what's going on?"

"Jack and Emily Ann weren't in the back room," I said. "The back door was standing open. I ran down to the park looking for them. Fortunately a friend found them over by the library and brought them back."

Rebecca pinned an expression of shock across her face. "Oh my goodness," she said. "I had no idea. Oh, the dear little things could have been killed. But you don't think that I—" She broke off, and laid her right hand theatrically upon her heart. "Why Louisa, you don't honestly think I opened that door, do you? I would never—"

I broke in, "Since they have never been able to open a door before this by themselves, yes, I do think."

"But—" She turned to Kay. "Are you going to let her talk to me like this?

Kay intervened. "Louisa, you're upset. Maybe the door didn't get shut all the way earlier and they nosed it open. Now, you're all muddy. Go upstairs and change clothes and calm down. I know it was really

93

scary to find they were gone."

I glared at her. I didn't believe they'd opened the door themselves, and for Kay to defend Rebecca made me want to pin her to the floor as well. But I couldn't spend one more second near Rebecca.

Without another word I walked around the counter and through the door to the back room, dogs at my heels. Behind me I heard Kay making soothing noises to Rebecca. At the foot of the stairs I paused and bent over to untie the strings from the dogs' collars. Straightening, I looked through the open risers of the stairway toward Kay's desk and saw the two purses where I had dropped them only a few minutes earlier.

I grabbed the purses and ran up the stairs, propelled by the last of my adrenaline and anger. The dogs followed. At the landing I unlocked the door into Kay's place, closed the door behind us, then sank down on the floor.

Jack and Emily Ann crowded around me once more, wagging and snuffling and stepping on purses. It was pure comfort. My shoulders went down a notch.

"Did that bad Rebecca push you outside?" I asked them. Not for the first time I wished we spoke the same language so they could tell me what had happened. Emily Ann gave me one more little smooch, then took herself over to Kay's sofa and laid down on it with a sigh. Jack sat next to me and leaned. "At least you're all right. Heck, you probably had a great time." Jack thumped his tail in agreement. "Good thing Hank was around to rescue you. Were you heading to the library for something to read? Or did you think this was the day for storytime?"

The mud on my slacks caught my attention, and I levered myself off the floor. I kept a few pieces of clothing in the small second bedroom. Jack jumped up on the bed and made himself comfortable while I pulled on a pair of ancient jeans. The cream linen blouse I'd put on that morning to work in the store looked as good with jeans as the brown slacks I'd taken off, so I kept it on. I rolled the slacks into a ball to take home and launder, then looked at my watch. Almost a quarter to three. I'd ask Kay if she needed me, and if not I'd go by the grocery store. If Hank was going to help me unpack boxes, or perhaps even mow the lawn, I'd need more food in the house than some stiff cheese and a few stale crackers. I was tired of them myself.

The two purses were where I'd dropped them by the door. I put Kay's on her kitchen counter, then picked up my own.

"Come on, dogs, let's go ask Auntie Kay if we can leave early."

Emily Ann rose from the couch, and she and Jack stepped onto the landing outside Kay's door. They waited for me to close it behind us. I started down the stairs, holding my purse in one hand and the muddy slacks in the other. The dog's toenails clicked on the wooden steps as they followed me.

It happened seven steps from the bottom. One second I was trotting quickly down the familiar stairs. The next I felt something catch at my ankle. Then I was flying. I seemed to stay airborne a long time as the world turned in slow motion. I had plenty of time to watch the concrete floor rise to meet me.

11

"Louisa? Can you hear me?" Kay's voice was far away. I wanted to ignore it, but a lifetime's experience has taught me that Kay cannot be ignored. I sometimes suspect she was a terrier in her last life. "Louisa?"

I opened my eyes. Kay's face was inches from mine, with Emily Ann's and Jack's faces on each side of hers. They could have been a three-headed mythological beast, with identical worried expressions.

"What?" I mumbled. Above Kay I dimly saw the ceiling of the back room of her store. It was fuzzy and out of focus. I seemed to be lying on the floor.

Kay pulled her face away, taking the dogs with her. Her expression changed to one of relief. "Thank heavens," she murmured.

I tried to sit up, but a flash of pain stopped me. I'm not big on pain. And I had no clear sense of where this pain originated. Maybe everywhere.

"Don't move," Kay said. "The paramedics are on the way. Everything's going to be fine."

I closed my eyes again. The word paramedics could have nothing to do with me, but a little rest would be good. I started to drift away. Kay's voice came again, sharper.

"Louisa, stay with me," she commanded.

I frowned. Hadn't she told me recently that I couldn't stay with her, that I had to stay at my house and unpack boxes? I opened my eyes again.

"What about the boxes?" I asked.

"There aren't any boxes, honey. Just hang on till the ambulance gets here."

Something must be wrong with Kay. She knew perfectly well I had dozens of boxes waiting to be unpacked. But if she needed an ambulance, that would explain it. I'd just have to be patient with her.

"Okay," I agreed. "No boxes. Right."

Behind her, two tall figures appeared. Perhaps they only looked tall because I was lying on the floor. Kay stood up to talk to them, and Jack moved closer to me. One of the tall figures started to squat down beside me, then moved away again when Jack growled. Good old Jack. He'd keep me safe.

Kay grabbed Jack by the collar and tugged. Reluctantly he let himself be pulled away. "I'll put them upstairs," I heard her say. "Emily Ann, come on." Then she and both dogs were gone, and a strange face was in front of mine. It had deep brown eyes and a truly magnificent mustache. I guessed it was a man.

"So, been practicing your swan dive, have you?" The voice was deep and velvety.

"No," I said. What a ridiculous idea.

The man laughed. "Right. No practice needed. Can you tell me your name?"

"Louisa McGuire. Who are you?"

"I'm Jack Cordell." I relaxed. If this was Jack, I knew I'd be okay. "We're going to get you onto a stretcher and then take you for a little ride. It looks like you've broken your arm, and the next few minutes won't be much fun. But you've also hit your head and are probably concussed. I don't want to knock you out before a doctor sees you. You ready?"

"Hank is coming over to help me with the boxes," I confided. "But we can't get the lawn mower started."

"That Hank's a great guy," Jack said. He stood up.

I closed my eyes. I heard his voice from somewhere above me, but listening was too much trouble. I felt hands on both sides of me. The cold of the concrete floor disappeared as I began to float upward. Then I was blown away the pain.

12

"I'm fine," I told the nurse each time she woke me up, all night long, to make sure my concussion had not killed me in my sleep.

"I'm fine," I assured the doctor on his rounds in the morning, after I realized this was indeed the doctor and not a high school kid volunteering for some community service hours. "I'm ready to go home."

He nodded. "We'll see about getting you released later this morning. Do you have someone to stay with you? That was a pretty nasty knock on the head, and a broken arm takes some adjusting to."

"Yes, of course, I'll be well looked after."

An hour later the phone rang. This time it was Bob. "I'm fine," I said once again. "Really."

"How can you be fine? You're in the hospital and you have a broken arm." His voice was harried. I appreciated his concern, but it was an effort to find the energy to allay his fears.

Deep breath. "They're releasing me this morning, so I'm just hanging around the hospital. That's different from actually being in it. I'll just go home and take it easy for a few days and my arm will heal and I'll be back to normal."

I could hear his smile. "Normal might be a tiny overstatement. Seriously, Louisa, do you want me to come back? Kay said it was quite a fall."

Bob home again. Very tempting. "I'm fine," I insisted. "How are you, anyway? I loved the tape of your radio show, you were so—so authoritative."

"Thanks. It was all I could do to remember to breathe. Did it really sound okay?"

"It was great. So what are you doing next?"

"Well, if you're absolutely sure I don't need to come and soothe your fevered brow..." His voice trailed off.

"I'm sure." My voice was so firm I almost convinced myself.

"Then we're leaving this afternoon for Guatemala. We're going to do a piece on a traditional healer who uses hypnosis. If it turns out like we hope we think it will end up on NPR."

"Wow! I said you were going to be a star."

"Nah, the healer is the star, but the thing is, we'll probably be out of touch for a week or more. And it doesn't feel right to not even call you when you're in the hospital."

"I'm not in the hospital, I'm just—"

"—hanging around, I know," he finished. "I also know you probably wouldn't tell me if you'd been killed by falling down the stairs, let alone broken your arm."

"Definitely. Whenever I get killed I don't notify

anyone. Even you."

"That's fair. But I still—"

The door to my room opened and Kay bustled in. She was carrying the bag she bought when she started going to a gym. "Hey, cuz, you ready to get out of here?"

"Hang on," I said into the phone, "Kay's here." To her I said, "I'm talking to Bob."

"Oh, good, let me talk to him a second, will you?" She came over to the bed and took the phone out of my hand. "Hey, Jungle Jim, what did she say? ...Uh huh...I told you. She got all the stubborn genes in the family." She listened for several moments, then laughed. "You got that right. Don't worry, we'll take good care of her...Right. Listen, you be careful in the jungle, they have snakes and things...Okay, here she is."

She put the receiver back into my hand. I could hear Bob talking as I raised it to my ear.

"What?" I asked.

"I just don't feel right about being out of touch," he said, an unhappy note in his voice.

I stopped myself from sighing. Not helpful. "I know, I'd feel the same way if it were you with the broken bone. But I'll probably have to beat off helpers with my good left arm, and all I really want to do is go home and snuggle with Jack and Emily Ann. It's okay, really."

I glanced at Kay, who had wandered to the window and was looking out. I lowered my voice. "I really have been missing you though," I whispered.

102

"What? Sorry, I can't hear you, Louisa." He raised his voice and I held the phone away from my ear. "I think the connection has gone bad."

I gave up on the endearments. "That's okay, just take care of yourself and call me as soon as you get back, okay?"

When he disconnected, I handed the phone back to Kay to hang up. Before she could ask, I said firmly, "I'm fine."

"Yeah, right." I could tell she didn't believe me. "I brought you some clothes, and they told me you can check out when you're ready. Let's get you dressed."

She plopped the gym bag on the bed next to me and drew out undies, a pair of sweat pants, and a stretchy cardigan that was streaky with age. From the bottom of the bag came socks, sneakers, and a pair of sewing scissors. I look at this last object blankly.

"Are you planning to give me a haircut before I go home?"

"No, silly, I'm planning to make this sweater fit over your cast."

The next few minutes were exhausting. I'd broken an arm once before, but I had relegated that memory to a corner of my mind, along with a lot of other Roger-baggage. I had forgotten how awkward it made everything. And I'd never told Kay about the earlier time, so I had to remember not to refer to it. Watching what I said was as tiring as getting clothes on my body.

But at last I was sufficiently covered to go out in public. I sat down on the edge of the bed while Kay gathered my belongings and put them in the bag.

"We'll get you home in just a few minutes, and settled in your room. You can just snooze the rest of the day," Kay said. "Where's your cell phone? You can call me downstairs if you need anything."

I felt puzzled and wooly brained. Why would Kay be downstairs? "Are you going to stay in my guest room?" I asked her.

She looked at me blankly. "What? No. I'm taking you to my place. I'll be downstairs in the shop part of the time. Rebecca's holding the fort but you know how busy it's been."

Alarm fizzed up my spine. Rebecca. Kay's apartment, up the wooden stairs. "No. I want to go home."

She dropped the bag and put her hands on her hips. "What are you talking about? Of course you're coming home with me."

"Thank you, but no. I want to go home."

"And who's going to take care of you?"

"I don't need taking care of. I just want to go home to my own bed. When I feel like being up I'll sit quietly and watch movies or read. I'll be fine."

"You had a concussion. You shouldn't be alone. You're coming to my place." She set her jaw.

"A concussion doesn't last forever. I'm going home."

We glared at each other. We had actually inherited equal shares in the stubborn gene from our common ancestors, in spite of what she'd told Bob.

The door opened, and Hank walked in. He stopped short when he saw our expressions, then squared his shoulders and smiled.

"Mrs. McGuire," he said, "I've just heard about your accident and came to make sure you're all right. How are you?"

"I'm fine," I declared. "In fact, I'm going home as soon as my cousin gets me released. Oh, you haven't met each other, have you? Hank, this is my cousin Kay Chelton. Kay, Hank has been working on the yard for me, and is going to help with the unpacking."

Hank stepped forward to shake hands with Kay. "Nice to meet you," they said simultaneously. Hank smiled at her. Kay's answering smile was brief.

Hank turned to me. "What happened? You were fine when I saw you in the park and returned the dogs to you."

"I fell down the stairs at Kay's shop. She has a very hard floor in her back room."

"How did you fall? Did you trip on something?"

"I—I don't know. I can't remember."

Kay instantly looked alarmed. "What? You have amnesia?"

"Oh, I hope so. I've always wanted to have amnesia."

Hank laughed, then tried to turn it into a cough. Kay ignored him. "What's the last thing you remember?" she asked.

"From yesterday? I went up to your apartment after I got the dogs back from Hank, and changed clothes. Then I started downstairs, and then I was lying on the floor."

"You don't remember how you fell?" Kay looked troubled.

I started to shake my head, but pain from the concussion awoke. "No, I don't."

"Rebecca said that the dogs tripped you."

"No. They couldn't have."

"Why not? They were coming down the stairs with you."

"We go up and down those stairs all the time. They always follow me. They do not push past me."

"She was putting the mail on my desk when you came down the stairs. She said they tripped you."

Suddenly I found it hard to breathe. Rebecca had been near the stairs when I fell.

"Maybe the dogs saw her and were hurrying down the stairs." The worried look remained on Kay's face. She shook her head. "However it happened, you need looking after. You can't fall on your head and break your arm and then just go home alone."

Back to that again.

I could not go back to Kay's place.

"I'll be fine. It's not like I'm going to the Antarctic or something."

Hank shifted his weight from one foot to the other and spoke diffidently. "Perhaps I could be of help."

Kay gave him a measuring look. "What do you mean?"

"I was planning to be at Louisa's—Mrs. McGuire's—house anyway, to unpack boxes. I can do that and handle any fetching and carrying that's needed, and I'm a pretty good cook. And, um..." His voice trailed off and he looked at me. "I've just found out that the room I've been renting is no longer available, so I was going to have to find another place to live. Perhaps I could stay in your guest room for a couple of nights. Just until you're feeling more the thing and I've found a new place. I promise I don't leave wet towels on the bathroom floor, and I won't steal the silver or anything."

"It's a deal," I said quickly, before Kay could get her mouth open.

Home again. My sofa had never looked so inviting. I stifled a little moan of relief as I sank into its welcoming cushions. Like the frog messenger in *Alice in Wonderland*, I planned to remain here for days and days and days. That thought reminded me.

"When you're unpacking stuff," I said to Hank, "keep an eye out for an ugly frog. I can't remember what I did with it."

He looked up from where he knelt on the floor petting Jack. "Frog?"

"Yeah, it's this stupid frog figurine, about this big." I held my hands a few inches apart. "I'm sure I brought it home and put it somewhere and I just can't remember."

"I guess concussions will do that," he said wisely. "Is it valuable?"

"Can't blame losing it on the concussion, I'd already forgotten where I put it before I fell down the stairs. And no, it's not valuable. At least I don't think so. It's heavy but feels like plastic and has a stupid crown on its head. Some guy gave it to me by mistake at the flea market."

His face was bent toward Jack again, and his voice came out a bit muffled. "Sure, I'll keep an eye out for it. Are you comfortable? Can I bring you anything?"

"I'd love one of the pillows from my bed, and the afghan on the bench in there, thanks."

Soon I was settled in, with Emily Ann curled into an impossibly tiny circle at my feet and Jack keeping vigil on the floor beside the sofa. I drifted off into sleep to the whispered lullaby of books coming out of boxes and settling onto their shelves.

13

The next day callers arrived, all intent upon bringing me comfort and cheer and finding out how I had come to fall down Kay's stairs. Dan was the first, fresh from the dog park. I had just finished breakfast and was still at the table, glancing through the newspaper and nursing another cup of tea. Emily Ann and Jack jumped up and barreled downstairs just before the doorbell rang. Hank hurried after them. I heard the low rumble of male voices in greeting. I combed my fingers through my hair and sat up straighter.

The dogs erupted back up the circular stairs, accompanied by Dan's dog Roxie, who came directly to me and laid her head in my lap. I stroked her brow and felt soothed. In a moment Dan appeared.

"Louisa!" he said, sitting down at the table across from me. "This is a hell of a thing. Can I sign your cast?"

"You could if I had the faintest idea where a marking pen might be. But I don't. We're still unpacking."

"Dang, woman, you ought to be done with that by

now."

"I know, I know. How was the dog park this morning?"

"Damp," he responded. "Heavy dewfall last night. You'd have needed those gardening boots you got. That little poodle of Mrs. Johnson's was a mess."

Hank returned from downstairs. "May I offer you a cup of coffee, sir? Or tea?"

"You got coffee? I know Louisa is probably drinking that other swill." He peered over at my cup.

"Swill, indeed," I said, trying to look offended. "Roxie, go bite that man for me." She lifted her head from my lap, looked searchingly at my face, then went to Dan and flopped down on his feet. He laughed.

"Good girl, Rox," he said, leaning over to give her shoulder a pat.

"Coffee it is," drawled Hank, and went to the kitchen.

In a few minutes he was back with a steaming mug. "Can I get either of you anything else? No? I'll get back to the unpacking then." He moved over to the living room and pried open a box.

"So what was the big idea? You tired of working for your cousin?" Dan asked. He dumped a heaping spoonful of sugar from the bowl on the table into his coffee and stirred vigorously.

"I just wanted to be the center of attention for a while. Falling downstairs seemed like the safest bet," I said. We grinned at each other.

"Yeah, right. You need to watch those drama queen tendencies, Louisa, or you'll hurt yourself one of these days."

"You have a point," I admitted.

"Seriously, what happened? Someone said you tripped over Emily Ann."

At least this I could deny. "Absolutely not. I was going down the stairs like I have a million times, the dogs were behind me, and suddenly I was getting to know Kay's floor really, really well." I thought about mentioning Rebecca, but held the words back. With my luck she'd find out and sue me for slander.

"Could one of the dogs have bumped you from behind?"

I shook my head. "I honestly can't remember exactly what happened, but I just don't think so. They always follow me down the stairs. They don't pass me or run ahead. You know what creatures of habit dogs are."

"That's because you're the leader of their pack," he said, nodding wisely. "It's a damned shame. You're lucky you weren't hurt worse. Your timing sucks, though. If you'd done it a few weeks earlier, we could have sold your discarded cast at the auction."

"Oooh, ig!" I wrinkled my nose at the thought. "I'm sure someone would really have forked over a pile of cash for my disgusting used cast."

"Maybe we could have gotten someone famous to autograph it."

"How are the auction plans coming?"

"Good," Dan nodded. "We can still use more donations, but it's coming along."

"I had hoped to donate this ugly frog thing," I told

him, "but I can't find it."

A metallic crash resounded from the living area. "Sorry," Hank called, "I dropped a tray."

"Not to worry," I called back. To Dan I said, "Even before I fell down the stairs I was losing my mind. I thought I brought this frog figurine home, and I can't find it anywhere. It's so ugly I don't want it, but it makes me a bit crazy to have no memory of what I did with it. And no, it wasn't the fall that caused it, I'd already forgotten before I fell."

"Don't worry about it too much," Dan soothed. "I lost my memory years ago and haven't missed it a bit."

We chatted a few more minutes before he rose to go. "I'm sure glad you didn't do yourself in," he said. "Your funeral would have been more competition than our auction could stand."

"Maybe you could have combined them. Even the non-dog lovers would have come for the spectacle of a combined funeral and dog park auction."

He laughed. "That's a thought. Bet we could have got that on TV and really cleaned up. But hey, it's still a few days off."

"Don't get your hopes up," I said, shaking my head. "I plan to be very careful from now on."

Hank followed Dan and Roxie downstairs to let them out, and I heard their voices recede as they went out into the yard. When Hank didn't return right away, I rose from my chair and went to the window overlooking the yard. Hank was speaking earnestly to Dan, who nodded, then both men walked toward the shed. I watched as Hank opened the door and pulled out the lawn mower. The next few minutes were a pantomime of frustration, as they took turns trying to start the machine. It remained stubbornly silent. Dan finally shook his head and shrugged. They shook hands, then Hank turned back toward the house. I hurried back to my seat at the table and picked up the paper once more. When Hank came back upstairs I was engrossed in an article about a naked motorist who crashed into seventeen other cars.

Hank had barely returned to the box he was working on when Eileen, another Maple Street merchant, showed up, and after that it was Earlene, my real estate agent. Earlene brought a plate of cookies still warm from the oven.

"I wish I could claim I had baked them myself, but it was Gina." Gina is Earlene's sister. "I was out with Felicia Bonneville to look at a condo for her daughter who's getting married in August, and my cell phone started vibrating. You know, Louisa, that I don't like to take phone calls when I'm with a client. That is just so rude. So I ignored it, figured whoever it was would leave a message. But then it buzzed again. I had it in my pocket, and about every two minutes it went off. By the seventh or eighth time I knew it had to be Gina. I could hardly think straight with that thing acting like it was about to bite me every few seconds. I finally dropped off Felicia and checked for messages and after all those calls there was not one message so then I knew it was Gina for sure. I called her back and started to tell her to just leave a message and not keep calling and before I got a word out she told me to get over there to pick up these cookies for you. I hope you like cranberries. She's the only person I ever knew who puts cranberries in her chocolate chip cookies."

The cookies were delicious. Earlene and I polished off a few before the doorbell rang again. This time Hank ushered Mrs. Johnson up the stairs, Prince Henri snuggled in her arms. He was dry and fluffy, so she must have been home and worked on him with the hair dryer after their trip to the dog park.

"Mrs. McGuire, Miss Hofenstadter," she said with a regal inclination of her head. I leapt to my feet, wincing when I banged my cast on the edge of the table.

"Mrs. Johnson! Please come in. Um, why don't we sit over here." I gestured toward the sofa and chairs in the living area. Somehow I could not see Ed's mother sitting at my kitchen table.

Hank materialized and picked up the plate of cookies. "Let me put these on the coffee table. Mrs. Johnson, would you care for some tea? Coffee?"

"Nothing, thank you."

Earlene rose. "I must be off. Another appointment soon. Nice to see you, Mrs. Johnson. Louisa, you take care of yourself."

She headed downstairs, with Hank following. Mrs. Johnson settled onto the stiffest of my chairs and settled the poodle on her lap. He looked around with bright eyes. "Edward told me about your accident. What a frightening experience."

"It happened so quickly I had no time to feel anything but surprise." I lowered myself onto the sofa and leaned back against the cushions.

"What caused you to fall?"

I explained yet again that I didn't know what had made me tumble down the stairs, ignoring the conversation going on in my head. The grumpy voice said darkly, that's a lie if I ever heard one. The indignant one insisted, we know perfectly well it was *not* the dogs. Even the sane one agreed, putting in tartly, you'll never prove it, but it was Rebecca. To keep from blurting any of this aloud, I said, "Dan stopped by earlier. He said you were at the dog park this morning."

She almost smiled. "Yes, Prince Henri now insists that we go every morning. Some of the dogs are rather rough, but he seems to enjoy their romping."

"He's certainly able to hold his own," I agreed. "And he runs rings around most of them."

She looked down at him proudly and stroked his topknot. "I must admit the exercise is good for him. Otherwise I fear he'd be running rings around me."

I blinked. I'd never heard her say anything even faintly humorous. Before I could come up with a reply, the doorbell rang again. Hank was still downstairs; I heard the door open and he greeted someone. "Mrs. McGuire is upstairs. May I carry your box for you?"

Footsteps rang on the stairs and a tall middle aged woman with a stunning figure appeared.

"Louisa!" she exclaimed. "You haven't changed a bit, I'd have known you anywhere."

Her voice was familiar. I connected it with the telephone. Of course. "Joan Stillman. How nice to see you. Do you know Mrs. Johnson?"

"I don't think we've met." Joan smiled at the older

woman and seated herself on the other end of the sofa. "You're Ed's mother, yes? I've heard so much about you from Kay."

Before the silence caused by this statement could get too long, Hank arrived carrying a medium-sized cardboard box, which he set on the coffee table in front of the sofa. "Would anyone like coffee? Tea?" he asked.

"You wouldn't have any iced tea, would you?" Joan asked. "The AC in my car is on the fritz and I'm about roasted."

"Certainly. Anyone else?" He headed for the kitchen. I watched him go, thinking that perhaps what I'd always needed was a butler.

Joan did indeed look warm. She flapped the front of her sleeveless linen blouse against her chest a few times. "Now that the flea market is over, I may have time to get my car fixed. I know my family is looking forward to having something for dinner besides take-out or boxed macaroni."

"Joan was in charge of the flea market in High Cross," I explained to Mrs. Johnson. "It was a particularly stressful planning process this year." To Joan I remarked, "Mrs. Johnson was at the market too."

"Oh, great! I hope you didn't get tangled up in the mess in the parking lot." She turned to me. "Louisa, remember I told you about the old man who had the stroke?"

I nodded. Mrs. Johnson said, "Stroke?"

"Yes, an elderly gentleman who was there by himself. And the parking lot was such a mess the emergency vehicles couldn't get through."

"How—how awful," Mrs. Johnson said.

"He's still not doing very well," Joan reported. "We finally figured out that the big old Cadillac that was left in the parking lot must be his. We were able to contact a family member to come get it, and they wanted to know if his dog was still in the car! Which of course it wasn't. We're just hoping he'll pull through. They seem to think he's fretting over what's become of his dog, and no one knows where it is." She smiled at Mrs. Johnson. Anyway, I'm glad you came over for the market. Did you find anything good?"

I was astonished to see a wave of pink suffuse Mrs. Johnson's cheeks. She sounded quite flustered as she said, "I—I picked up one or two items while I was there. Some, er, linens." The diamonds on her wedding ring flashed as she tightened her hold on Prince Henri. "I'm afraid I must be going. So nice to have met you. Mrs. McGuire, I'm glad that you're recovering from your experience."

She stood, and before I could say anything she hurried to the stairs, her back ramrod straight as she descended. I heard the front door open and close again.

"Well!" said Joan, looking after her with wide eyes. "Was it something I said?"

"Oh, no, she's just like that," I assured her. But I'd never seen Mrs. Johnson move so precipitously before, and I couldn't help wondering why she had fled.

Hank returned with a glass of iced tea on a tray, probably the tray he'd dropped earlier. He set the glass next to the plate of cookies on the coffee table.

"Your other guest left?" he asked, looking around.

"She—had somewhere to be." I reached for a cookie. "So, Joan, what's in the box?"

"Frogs! I brought you all those frogs for your auction. I called Kay and she told me about your fall, so I figured I'd better deliver them."

Hank lowered himself to the floor and opened the flaps of the box, then looked at me. "May I?"

"Sure."

He reached into the box and brought out a frog. It was of clay, with three holes in the top and another in the region of its butt. Hank chuckled. "It's an ocarina." He put it to his lips and blew a few notes.

"If you'll come play it at the auction, I'm sure it will sell," I told him.

"I'm afraid you've now heard my entire repertoire." He set the ocarina on the table and reached into the box again. The frog that appeared was made of green satin, and had wings and a unicorn's horn. We all looked at it, but no one found anything to say. The next frog to appear was clearly a child's toy, attached to a long tube that ended in a round plastic device that made it jump when pressed.

"This is quite a collection," I remarked. Hank kept pulling out frogs, each more eccentric than the last.

"He had even more," Joan said. "When that weird woman shoved them all off the table, some of the china ones broke."

"Oh. Too bad," I said. We all three burst out laughing.

Joan stayed for about half an hour, reminiscing

about people we'd gone to school with, most of whom I had forgotten. There was a lull in visitors after she left, then more acquaintances arrived. Some were people from the dog park, others were friends of Kay's. Kay herself stopped in for a few minutes to see how I was doing. Earlene's cookies ran out and were replaced by offerings ranging from homemade coffee cake to a plastic tray of cheese slices from the Food Right.

By six I was exhausted. I almost regretted that I had resisted going to Kay's place. She would have refused to let everyone in town up the stairs to see me. "I think it's time to pull up the drawbridge," I told Hank from my corner of the sofa. "Let's have a bowl of the soup Dorothy brought over and then I'll go fall down for the night."

He was instantly contrite. "I'm sorry, I should have seen how tired you are and kept people away. Let me get you some dinner."

"It was good to have the distraction," I assured him. "Probably kept me from falling downstairs again over and over in my head."

"Then perhaps it was worth it."

"Tell you what. If you'll put the soup on the stove to heat, I'll stir it while you go check the mail. The box is at the end of the drive."

"Of course." He went to the kitchen. In a few moments he was back. "Okay, soup's on, as they say. I turned the flame down, and I'll hurry. You rest here and I'll bring your supper on a tray as soon as I get back with the mail."

"Thanks, that would be great. If you want to let the dogs walk along, just tell them to sit and stay before they reach the road. I think they're smart enough not to get run over but I'd hate to be wrong."

"Sit and stay it is," he agreed cheerfully, and waved as he descended the stairs, both dogs following.

I settled back and thought what a nice young man he was. Even though he obviously knew nothing about mowing I was glad he'd shown up on my doorstep. I hoped that someday I'd be able to tell his mother what a great job she'd done with him.

I must have dozed off, because a burning smell brought me to attention. I scrambled off the sofa and hurried to the kitchen, where the soup had gotten hot enough to boil over.

I turned off the flame and moved the pan, then frowned. Where the heck was Hank? I'd told him not to hurry, but he'd been gone—I glanced at the clock—almost fifteen minutes. The voices in my head went into overdrive.

"Men!" said the caustic one. "They have no sense of time!"

"Maybe he got run over by a truck," said the worrier.

"Not too many trucks on this road," the sane one tried to be reassuring.

I headed down the stairs to check on him nonetheless.

"Maybe he was just waiting for a chance to steal Jack and Emily Ann!" said the voice with the lurid imagination. All the other voices scoffed. I tuned them out as I hurried out the door and down the drive. I was tired and my arm ached and I did not want to walk down the hill and back up again. I was grumbling in annoyance as I rounded the curve. I stopped short.

Hank was lying on the ground, face down. There was no sign of either dog. I ran to Hank and dropped to my knees beside him.

"Hank! Oh, Hank, what happened?" I wittered. He didn't move. I put out a shaking hand to feel for a pulse at his neck. I found it, strong and regular. The breath I didn't know I was holding whooshed out. "Hank, wake up," I commanded.

No response. I felt his cheek, I'm not sure for what. Maybe a sudden fever had knocked him off his feet. Then I ran a hand over his head. As I encountered a lump on the back of his skull, he groaned. "Hank?" I said again.

Another groan, and he moved. He braced one hand on the ground and pushed, rolled over. He open his eyes in a squint.

"Bloody hell," he said in a distinctly British accent, "the buggers have bashed me."

14

"A car was at the bottom of the drive. One of the back doors was open," Hank said, sinking onto the sofa and leaning back. He winced when his head touched the cushions. "Ouch."

"Hold on, I'll get some ice to put on that," I said. "Then we'd better get you to a doctor." Oh, for the days when doctors made house calls, I thought. I wouldn't have minded a bit of doctorly attention myself. Getting back to the house had left both of us white-faced and shaky.

"Ice, yes, doctor, no," Hank muttered. "It's just a bit of a bump. I'm fine."

"I've heard that before somewhere." I went around the corner to the kitchen and laid a dish towel on the counter. The icemaker was full; I grabbed a handful of cubes and plunked them on the towel. I folded it up with my left hand, then pinned it with my cast while I struggled to slip a rubber band around the lumpy bundle. I was already tired of that cast, and it was only the second day.

Back in the living room, Hank took the makeshift icepack from me and held it to the back of his head. I sat down in the rocker across from him.

"A car in the driveway?" I prompted.

"It was parked with one of the back doors open, right down at the end near the road. I didn't see anyone in it, but it had tinted windows so I can't be sure. Didn't see it until I went around the bend. The dogs ran ahead, and then they both hopped inside the car."

"That is odd," I said, frowning. "Though they do love to ride. Maybe it belonged to someone they know. It wasn't a red sports car, was it?"

"No, gray I think."

"I wonder if they smelled food or something."

"I couldn't see in past the tinted windows. Maybe someone was inside and called to them."

"This is so weird."

"I wasn't really worried about the dogs, but I picked up the pace to get them out. I mean, you never know if someone will be shirty about having two unknown dogs in their car."

"True."

"Then just as I passed those bushes with the purple flowers, I heard a noise. Before I could turn around whoever it was must have given me a bloody great wallop on the head." He shifted the icepack and winced.

"I didn't see or hear any cars."

"Probably drove off as quick as they could. I

daresay it took you a few minutes to come looking for us."

"Right. So by the time I arrived, the car and the dogs were gone. Why would anyone kidnap my dogs? This is ridiculous. It's not like they're valuable show animals." Something I'd read somewhere occurred to me. "Oh my god, you don't think they've been taken to a lab, do you? They do unspeakable things to dogs in labs. I've got to call Ed and—" I launched myself from the chair and turned toward the phone.

"No, no, I'm sure it's nothing like that." For some reason, his new English accent lent weight to his words. I sat down again.

"But where can they be?" This came out suspiciously like a wail. I caught my bottom lip between my teeth.

"Don't worry, we'll find them. I have an idea about where they might have gone." He saw the sudden hope on my face. "Okay, not where so much as who—"

"Where? Who? What's going on?"

The phone rang.

Most of the time I'm perfectly happy to let the answering machine pick up my calls. I like to know who's on the other end before I commit to talking to someone. But this time the shrill noise had me out of the chair again and picking up the receiver.

"Hello?"

Windy silence in my ear. "Hello?" I said again.

An overly loud metallic voice said, "Give us ze frog, or you weell never see zeese dogs again."

The accent was French, or faux-French. I squinted

in concentration.

"You have unteel tomorrow. Do not contact ze police. We weell call again with instructions."

A click, and the dial tone. I stood frozen with the receiver to my ear. Several heartbeats later I managed to hang up the phone. Hank stared at me.

"What?" he asked. "Who was it?"

"Emily Ann and Jack have been kidnapped by a French robot."

15

Hank's jaw dropped. "A—a French robot?" he repeated.

I fell into the chair I'd been sitting in earlier, banging my cast on its arm. "That's what it sounded like. A metallic voice with a French accent."

"What did the French robot say?"

Tears sprang to my eyes and cracked my voice. "I have to give them some frog by tomorrow or I'll never see the dogs again."

He closed his eyes as if in pain. "Was it a man's voice?"

"I couldn't tell. It really did make me think of a robot."

"Probably some kind of electronic distortion device. That and the accent would keep you from recognizing the voice, which means it's probably someone you've encountered before. Louisa, I cannot tell you how sorry I am that you've gotten mixed up in this."

My grief and fear for the dogs were swamped by a

126

surge of anger. "Mixed up in what? What the hell is going on? Who are you, anyway? First you're John Wayne and now you're Jeeves, and I don't think you've ever mowed a lawn in your life."

He turned bright pink. At any other time I'd have been entertained by the sight of so large a young man blushing like a Victorian maiden. "You're right. But I can explain—"

"I don't want explanations. I want my dogs back!" I wanted to throw back my head and howl. My expression must have been alarming, because Hank jumped to his feet, then stopped abruptly. The ice in his rudimentary pack tumbled to the floor.

"Ouch, my head," he said. He stood still for a moment, then knelt to pick up the scattered ice cubes. "Listen, neither of us had dinner, and it's been a long day. Let me serve the soup, and I'll tell you what I know, and we'll think of something. And if we don't then you can throw me out."

I wasn't sure I'd be able to swallow anything larger than a mashed pea, but I was too tired to argue. I nodded. In a few minutes Hank had placed two steaming bowls of Dorothy's soup on the table, and a plate of hot buttered toast. He came over to where I still slumped in my chair and held out a hand.

"Come, Louisa, let me help you to the table."

I ignored his hand. "I am not ninety three years old," I said crossly, even though I felt at least that age as I doddered to my feet. We sat across from each other. The soup smelled good. I ventured a bite, then another, and felt a little better.

"Okay, let's hear it. Start at any point that will clear things up. Maybe with who the hell you really are."

"My name really is Hank," he assured me. "Well, it's my nickname. Or one of them."

"Hank what? I suppose it's short for Henry."

He nodded. "Yes, Henry Padgell. Henry Beauchamp Lindley James Padgell, so you can see what an improvement Hank is."

"And we wouldn't want to confuse you with Prince Henri," I said. "Unless of course you are royalty, in which case I supposed you'd take precedence over a poodle."

He sipped a bit of soup. "No, not royalty," he said when he'd swallowed.

I stared at him. "What's that supposed to mean?"

"Just that I do have a sort of, um, title." He looked as though he were confessing to something embarrassing, like tripping over the Queen's corgi when invited to tea.

"You mean you're the Earl of Bagshot or something?"

"Something like that."

"Look," I commanded, "just tell me who the hell you are. You said you're not royalty so you can't be Prince what's his name.

"William?"

"Right. William."

"He'd never be in a mess like this. Harry might though." Hank said this as though he knew it for a fact. "I'm actually the Duke of Tintesford."

I goggled at him. "You're a *duke*?" He nodded. "Do you have a castle and ancestral lands and villagers pulling their forelocks at you?"

He snorted. "Hardly. You're a trifle out of date. I have an overly large house that eats up every cent I can lay my hands on, and the villagers think I'm still wet behind the ears. I love my home, but it's anyone's guess if I can hang onto it for another generation."

I softened a little. "Don't you have anyone to help you? Any family?"

The expression in his eyes was bleak. "Only my cousin Bernard, and he's been trying to kill me since I was two."

I couldn't stop the surprised snort that came out. "Hank! Surely not."

He nodded earnestly. "He was furious when I was born. He's fifteen years older than I, and had been raised to believe he would inherit the title. And then I came along. You see, our fathers were identical twins, but mine was born the crucial few minutes earlier."

"Seems like they would have to share."

"Doesn't work like that. Even though they were twins, they were very different people. My uncle was the proverbial extrovert, good at sports, good with women. He married young and produced Bernard. No one ever expected my father to marry at all. He was a scholar, always off somewhere in his head when he wasn't off on his researches. He met my mother when he was almost forty. Somehow she was able to see past his absent-minded-professor shell to the softie other people missed."

129

"What did Bernard do when you were two?"

"My parents were away and my nanny was called to the telephone. Bernard nipped in, picked me up, carried me to his car, and drove me out onto the moors, where he abandoned me."

"He just drove off and left you?"

"He did. It's one of my earliest memories."

"I take it someone found you."

"Bernard reckoned without my amazing capacity to make a fuss. I believe I played happily for a bit, but when I got hungry I started to howl. You could probably hear me for miles. At least a border collie did. I remember this black and white dog appearing out of nowhere and licking my face. You know dogs. Probably thought the tears and, well, snot were lovely."

I nodded. "Yup, that's the dogs I know. But it's been a while since you were two, and memories from that age are not always the most reliable."

"That wasn't the only time. Just the first. He's fairly determined but not very good at it."

"Thank heavens."

"And of course it has to look like an accident, or he won't inherit the title and all my worldly goods. And it's one of my worldly goods that has brought us to our present predicament."

"The frog."

"Right. The frog. That damned frog, if you will excuse my language."

"Hell yes," I said robustly.

He managed a small smile. "My great great grandfather was an amateur archeologist who spent years in Egypt, working on various excavations and doing his own exploring. Not many rules back then, and he shipped literally tons of artifacts home. For instance, a stone sarcophagus decorates my garden."

"Must be cozy."

"Quite." Hank stood and picked up my now-empty glass and bowl. "More tea?"

"Sure."

The worrier in my head started squawking, "You can't make a duke get you more iced tea! It should at least be hot tea." I was too tired to pay any attention, and anyway the duke—if he really was a duke—had been unpacking my boxes all day. Hank returned with the tea and a plate of gluten-free cookies that Bethie had brought.

"Thanks," I said, picking up a cookie. I took a small bite, then laid it down again. "So what's with the frog?"

"It's frightfully valuable," he said simply. "And two years ago archeologists found its twin, so being one of a pair makes it even more so. When I saw an article about the other one, I knew I had to give mine back to the people of Egypt."

"Wait a minute," I said, sitting up straighter in my chair. "We can't be talking about the same frog that the guy at the flea market—goodness, was that your cousin?"

"Tall, smarmy accent, really white teeth? Yes, that was Bernard."

"Hmmm. But we can't be talking about the frog that he slipped into my package. No way is that one was hideously valuable. It was about the awfullest thing I've ever seen. To call it butt-ugly would be an insult to butts everywhere."

Hank frowned. "Tell me what it looked like."

I started to hold out my hands to indicate its size, but was hampered by the cast. "About five inches long, sort of an elongated shape with bumps on the back. It was some kind of plastic material, a mottled olive green and yellow. Oh, and a stubby crown on its head. And quite heavy for its size."

"Mine is certainly not olive green and yellow. God, has Bernard taken me in again? I was so sure he was telling the truth this time. He seemed terrified."

"Terrified? When?"

"The day he gave you the frog by mistake. I caught up with him as he was fleeing the jumble sale. He said he had given you the Egyptian frog by mistake, and the woman who was supposed to get it was threatening to kill him."

That tallied with what Joan had said. Another question occurred to me. "I didn't tell him who I was or where I lived, and I paid cash. How did you find me?"

"You mentioned having a greyhound and taking it to a dog park. I went online and did a search for dog parks within fifty miles, then started looking. The trouble is, Bernard probably did the same thing, or the woman he was working with. Emily Ann is pretty distinctive. I got lucky, you were actually at the park here when I came upon it. So I followed you."

Emily Ann's name brought me back to our present dilemma. "And now she's g-gone," I stammered. I didn't even try to keep the accusation out of my voice. Hank looked stricken.

"We'll get her back," he reiterated, "and Jack. *And* my stupid frog."

"I'm still not convinced the one your cousin gave me, the one I can't remember putting anywhere, is valuable. Don't you have a picture of it?"

"Not with me. Where did I see some paper? I could sketch it for you."

I knew there was paper somewhere. "Maybe in my desk, in the bedroom." I started to rise.

"Sit still, I'll go." Hank shot to his feet, then paused with a hand to his head. "Crikey, I keep forgetting."

"A fine pair of heroes we are," I said, not able to keep the bitterness out of my voice. "Hobbling around with a broken arm and a broken head between us."

He looked down at me and smiled. "Ah, but we're going to keep hobbling along no matter what, and we're going to win. That's why we're the heroes."

16

"I found it," Hank called from my bedroom. I heard the rustling of paper, then his footsteps returning.

The phone rang. I tensed—what if the dognapper was calling again?

"I'll get it," Hank said, then in his John Wayne voice went on, "Mrs. McGuire's residence...oh yes, just a moment." He peered around the corner at me, his hand over the mouthpiece of the phone. "It's your cousin," he hissed.

My shoulders went down. "Stretch that cord over here," I said, reaching out my left hand. "Hi, Kay."

"Hey, hon, how you doing? You were looking a little ragged this afternoon. Did everybody in town come by and wear you out? You think they'd have more sense. Listen, I was going to come over and help you get ready for bed, but I'm not going to make it. That committee I'm on has called an emergency meeting."

"The pedestrian bridge committee?"

"Right. They'll all be mad at me if I skip a meeting. I'm not sure what kind of emergency we could have for a bridge that hasn't been built yet, but Eileen insists I have to come. I'll be at Gloria Adams' house. I'll see you tomorrow. Will you be okay this evening?"

"Sure," I said.

"I could come over after the meeting, but you know how long these things can go one. Everyone has to say the same things nine times."

"I'll be fine."

"You get some sleep," she ordered. "Bye, hon, see you tomorrow."

"Bye," I agreed. She'd already hung up. I handed the receiver back to Hank. He looked amused.

"You didn't have much to say to her." He replaced the phone and sat down at the table.

"Sometimes you need a pretty nimble tongue with Kay, and I don't have it in me tonight. She was going to come over but now she's not. Which is good because I'd have to tell her about the dogs and then she'd tell Ed and they said no cops." I felt tears threatening again and bit my lip. "She, um, oh, she said she's going to a committee meeting at Gloria Adams' house."

"And who is Gloria Adams?" He held a pencil lightly and started sketching.

"She makes jewelry that she sells in a couple of the shops on Maple Street. Earrings and bracelets. She uses a combination of silver and—" I stopped, struck by inspiration. "Polymer clay!"

He looked up from his drawing, his expression uncertain. "That certainly sounds...uh, interesting." His

135

voice trailed off.

"No, no, I mean, that's it!"

"I beg your pardon?"

"Polymer clay! That's what was covering the frog! That mottled green and yellow. It felt like plastic, but the piece was so heavy I didn't see how it could be."

"And what is polymer clay when it's at home?"

"Oh, it's this craft material. A kind of clay but you don't need a kiln to fire it. You bake it right in your oven. People use it to make jewelry and dolls and decorative pieces."

He was looking interested. "So you think they could have covered the Egyptian frog with this stuff and baked it? Wouldn't that be dangerous for the frog? What if it had melted?"

"It wouldn't though, that's the thing. It bakes at a pretty low temperature. Something like three hundred degrees, or maybe less. Fahrenheit. I'm sure that gold wouldn't melt at that temperature. Pretty sure."

"You're probably right."

"Oh, and sometimes people use something like aluminum foil to make an armature and they cover it with the clay and then bake it."

"How do you know all this? Are you an artist?"

I shook my head. "No, but playing with clay is always fun, even when you're a grown up. Which is why, when I found a box of it at a yard sale last month, I bought it."

Our eyes met. "Are you thinking what I'm thinking?" Hank asked.

"Probably. We can't find the real frog, and we only

136

have until tomorrow to give it to the dognappers. Maybe we could buy some time by cooking up our own yellow and green frog and giving them that."

He looked both hopeful and skeptical. "But how? I mean, I'm no artist and you only have one working hand."

"You'll have to do it somehow," I told him firmly. "Maybe you could start with one of those other frogs that Joan brought over this afternoon. And maybe the dognappers don't know what the real one actually looks like."

His face fell. "They do if it's my cousin. He knows the Egyptian frog in its normal state as well as in its disguise."

"True." I drummed my fingers on the table. "But if your cousin didn't take the dogs, then we'd have a chance. If we can just get the dogs back, then we can tell Ed what's going on and keep looking for your frog."

"I suppose so." Doubt still shaded his voice.

"And if it is your cousin, then I say let's kidnap him and make him tell us where the dogs are. You're bigger than he is. Don't you want a chance to beat him up?" I suddenly felt quite bloodthirsty. If whoever had taken Emily Ann and Jack appeared before me at that moment I'd have had a good shot at laying them out with my left hand, or with the damned cast if need be.

Hank grinned at me. "I would love a chance to beat up Bernard. All right, we'll try it. Here's a rough sketch of the Egyptian frog. Does this look anything like the one you had?"

I took the paper he'd been drawing on and looked

137

at the elongated shape. Something stirred in my memory. "Kay said..." I squinted, trying to remember. "Something like, if you didn't look at the color and the crown it had interesting lines." I picked up the pencil with my left hand and drew a stumpy, and slightly wavering, crown. "That's it. It must have been your Egyptian frog. Now all we need to do is disguise another frog to look like the Egyptian frog in disguise."

"This is starting to have a definite wheels-within-wheels aspect. All right. We'll try. Where are the frogs Mrs. Stillman brought, and where is this clay stuff from your yard sale?"

I rubbed my forehead. "The frogs are still in the living room. The clay..." My voice trailed off.

"I know, you have no idea. With all due respect, Louisa, I suggest that you never move house again." The twinkle in his eyes removed any sting. "What does it look like? Maybe it was in something I unpacked but I didn't recognize it."

"It was in a small white box," I said, glad I could at least remember that much. "Cellophane wrapped squares, about ten different colors."

"Got it." He jumped to his feet, winced, hurried downstairs. I heard thumping noises, then he charged back. "I kept running across things I needed to ask you about when you were either asleep or talking to one of your visitors, so I stashed them in another box until you were free. Is this it?"

I nodded. "That's it."

"So how do we use it?"

"Fire up the computer," I told him, "and Google

polymer clay. I'm sure you'll find instructions on prepping and baking. And let's just hope this goes better than starting the lawnmower."

"Amen to that," he intoned, and headed for the computer.

17

I tried to pry my eyelids open, but they were glued fast with some gritty substance. My head did not want to lift from the odd position it was in, face down on my arms. My back seemed to have ossified. I stifled a groan. I was too old to fall asleep at the kitchen table.

More effort unstuck my eyes, but they closed again as soon as they focused. I was surrounded by frogs. Misshapen frogs, of various colors and sizes. Cautiously I peeked again. Some were dark, almost black. A powerful burned smell invaded my nostrils.

Fear that the house was on fire brought me upright, but apparently the smell was only our ill-timed experiments in frog making. I rubbed my eyes with my left hand and looked around. Hank had been hard at work after sleep had overtaken me.

The earliest attempts looked more pre-Columbian than ancient Egyptian, though maybe preschool would come closer to the mark. Lumpy blobs, vaguely amphibian shaped, covered with streaky polymer clay that in some cases had cracked and fallen off. The stumpy crowns he'd tried to attach to the tops had fallen off of some, and shards of baked clay littered the table.

This was hopeless. We'd never pull this off. No one would be fooled for a second by one of these monstrosities. We'd never find the real frog, either. I'd probably thrown it away with the bag it had been in. Probably now moldered in the town dump. Future archeologists would find it and make up stories about the strange civilization it had come from. And I'd never see Emily Ann and Jack again.

The thought brought a surge of mingled anger and despair. I stood up, gritting my teeth to keep the howl I could feel in my chest from erupting. The house was dim and silent. It must be very early morning. I wondered where Hank was.

A small snore gave me a clue. I softened at the sight of him sprawled over the sofa, sound asleep. His long arms and legs escaped the confines of the piece of furniture, and his face in repose had the innocence of a child's. It was odd to think that this overgrown specimen was actually a duke, and I marveled at the chance that had brought him to my doorstep.

From the evidence scattered over the kitchen table, he'd certainly tried hard to produce a fake Egyptian frog. Not his fault that none of the specimens even came close. I would just have to tell the dognapper when he or she or it called that I had lost the damned thing and beg for my dogs back. Substituting a fake as the ransom was a hare-brained idea anyway.

I tiptoed to the bathroom, acutely aware that no dogs were in the house to follow me as they usually did. A glance in the mirror revealed a face with drooping lines by the eyes, and hair that stuck up in tufts on one side of my head and mushed down on the other.

At least the cast they'd given me was one I could shower with. A few minutes under hot water made me feel a bit more alive. I let the water drip out of my cast as I'd been instructed. Then with my left hand I toweled off clumsily.

Looking in the mirror once more, I thanked heaven for short hair. Forgoing the blow dryer so as not to wake Hank, I flicked strands into place with the brush. No beauty contests would be won today, at least not by me, but at least I felt less sticky and a great deal more confident of my ability to take care of myself. I might not be able to start a lawn mower but I could at least wash and dry myself with one hand.

So there.

Dressing myself had to be approached in an analytic manner. Staying with Kay would have had some advantages, such as assistance in putting on a bra. Fortunately sports bras might have been invented with the one-handed in mind. I managed to wrestle one into place, though by the time it was on I had to sit on the edge of my bed to catch my breath. I felt old and exhausted and hot and my broken arm throbbed and no dogs flopped at my feet to make me feel better. I was mightily tempted to take one of the pain pills I'd been given when I checked out of the hospital, then crawl into bed and pull the covers over my head and stay there.

Hunger came to my rescue. My stomach gave a gurgle. "Get some breakfast," I commanded sternly, and it was enough to get me back on my feet.

I tiptoed past Hank, still sprawled over the sofa and snoring softly, to pull out a saucepan from a kitchen cupboard and start water heating for oatmeal. Comfort food was definitely the order of the day. Then I turned to the table with its litter of vague frog shapes. Red, purple, blue—the blue seemed to have been particularly prone to becoming scorched. Maybe he'd tried that last, when he was most tired.

Somehow it seemed churlish just to sweep all this effort into the trash. But one of the advantages of moving is that you have a ready supply of boxes on hand afterward. I heard the water in the saucepan begin to boil, so I added oatmeal and turned down the heat. Then I tiptoed into the living room to look for an empty box. I spotted a smallish one near the sliding door that opened to the deck.

When we had packed up my old house, we'd marked each box with a rough list of contents. This one, in Kay's bold print, read "Dog toys, shampoo, flea goop."

I had to get my dogs back.

The sound of a yawn made me turn, and Hank's tousled head appeared over the back of the sofa.

"Mornin', ma'am," he said in his best John Wayne drawl.

I accomplished a small smile. "Can I interest you in some oatmeal?"

"Brilliant." He reverted to his own voice. "Let me do it."

"Already cooking. Let's sit out on the deck."

"Great. Give me a minute and I'll set the table." He was on his feet and down the stairs. I took the box to the table and started putting in the various amphibious lumps, handling them with ridiculous care. Some were quite heavy for their size, so evidently he'd had some success with the weight requirement. If only any of them had actually looked like the Egyptian frog. Maybe we could have painted it, or dabbed it with magic markers.

The iron stairs rang with Hank's footsteps as he charged back upstairs. "So how do you like it?" he asked eagerly.

I stared at him. Like what? The oatmeal? The linen shorts and blue t-shirt he had put on? "Uh..." I temporized.

The phone rang. My heart skipped a beat or two as our eyes met and locked. Then I leapt across the room and grabbed the receiver. "Hello?"

"Hey, Louisa, I didn't wake you, did I?"

"Oh, Dan, hi. No, I was awake, you know me." My shoulders dropped several inches. "What's up?"

I heard barking in the background. "I'm at the dog park. Any chance you'll be coming down here today?"

He had a lot faith in my powers of recuperation.

144

"No, sorry, not today. I—I'm tied up this morning."

"Darn. Just doesn't feel the same without you and Emily Ann and Jack."

I was touched. And stabbed with longing once more for my dogs. "Maybe tomorrow. I hope."

"Take it easy today, then, and get down here tomorrow, you hear?"

"Hope so. Talk to you later."

"Later, gator."

"The French robot had better call soon," I sighed as I hung up, "because I'm going to have a heart attack every time the phone rings."

"As am I," Hank agreed. "Do you expect a lot of calls? Because if you are, it might be better if we took turns having our heart attacks."

"Everyone knows I hate the phone," I told him, "but that won't stop them."

As if on cue, the phone rang again. Since I was still standing beside it, I grabbed it on the first ring. "Hello?"

"Hey, hon, it's me."

"Kay. Hi." I looked at Hank and gestured toward the kitchen. "You're up early."

Hank went to the stove and stirred the cereal, then turned off the flame. He caught my eye and mouthed, "Lid?" I pointed to a lower cabinet.

"Stuff to do," Kay said cheerily. "Ambrose has a client from Kansas City he's bringing by at nine to look over some stuff. I just wanted to see how you're doing. How's the arm?"

"Itchy," I admitted. It also ached but Kay could do

145

nothing about that. Or about the itch.

"I don't suppose you'd like to come in to the store for a few hours today, would you? We could really have used you yesterday. Every tourist in the state showed up. You could just sit at the register and—"

"Oh, um, gosh Kay, I wish I could but..." But my dogs have been kidnapped and I'm waiting for a French robot to call me so I can ransom them with a fake Egyptian frog that I don't have and besides I can barely stand to be in the same county with Rebecca, let alone the same room.

Kay's voice was instantly contrite. "Of course not. I shouldn't have asked."

Guilt stabbed me. "No, no, it's just that, well, I'm sort of expecting a phone call and I'm not sure what time it will be and—"

"Bob's going to call? Great! I thought he was still in the jungle."

"No, I mean yes, he is, but—"

"I'll let you go. Tell him I said hi. And call me if you need anything."

"Okay, thanks." I hung up the phone, and before I could remove my hand it rang again. I gave an exasperated sigh. Kay does this all the time—thinks of one more thing to say and calls me right back. I've perfected the art of saying goodbye and hello on the same breath. "Yeah, now what?"

The receiver held a moment of startled silence, and then, "If you want to see zeese dogs again you weel do exactly as I say."

146

18

I gave an involuntary squeak and dropped the receiver, which hit the floor with a crash. As I reached down to pick it up, I whacked my cast on the wall by the phone. Dark specks floated in front of my eyes. I lost my balance and fell over, landing on one knee. I tried to right myself, and ended up on my butt. I leaned against the wall, took a deep breath and picked up the phone.

"Um, hello?" I quavered. "Are you still there?"

"*Oui, certainement.* Are you going to cooperate?"

"How—what do you want me to do?"

"You must bring ze object to a place I weel tell you. You weel leave it and return to your home. Your dogs weel be waiting for you when you return."

I didn't like this. "But I thought...I want you to give me the dogs as soon as I give you the frog."

The French robot gave a metallic laugh. "Right, and 'ave you tell them to attack."

"They're not attack dogs, they're pets," I protested.

"Zey may be pets, but I have read ze news reports

about thees black dog and how he attack a man with a gun," the robot replied. "No. You weel do as I zay."

The robot had me there. Jack had actually saved my life twice in the past year, and while he certainly was no attack dog, I had entertained some fantasies of what might happen when we exchanged the fake Egyptian frog for him and Emily Ann.

"I guess I have no choice," I said, aiming for coolness so that my voice wouldn't crack. "Where am I supposed to take the frog?"

"You weel travel east on ze River Road. You know zis street?"

"Of course."

"On the edge of town, you weel pass a gas station."

"The Texaco?"

"*Oui,* zat is ze one. Go another mile, and make ze right turn on Thompson Street into a neighborhood."

"Okay."

"Make two more right turns, then turn onto a dirt road to ze right and follow eet until you come to an old barn."

Unbelievable. This stupid robot was making me go back to the old barn where I'd nearly met up with a killer last October. "I've seen it before."

"Zat is where you weel leave ze frog. Put eet on the floor in ze lower area. Leave it at ten-fifteen thees morning. You must be absolutely alone. Eef anyone is weeth you, you weel never see zeese dogs again."

"Alone? But how am I supposed to get there?"

"Wot do you mean?" The robot gave a disgusted snort. "You weel drive yourself zere in your car."

"But I can't. I have a broken arm," I protested.

"Zo? Zeese ees not a cross country journey. I am sure you can drive yourself a few miles. Put ze car in Drive and go."

Good grief, said a disgusted voice in my head. Not just a robot with a fake French accent, but a stupid robot with a fake French accent.

"I can't do that," I insisted. "My car has a stick shift, and my right arm is broken. I don't suppose you want me to do something conspicuous like rent a sedan with an automatic. I have to have a driver. A friend is staying at my house and can drive me."

One second ticked by, then another, and another. "Yes..." the robot said slowly, "I zee. Yes, zat weel be quite all right." I would have sworn the voice was pleased. "Have heem drive you, and do not be late. And remember—" a note of threat entered the metallic voice—"we weel be watching you ze entire time. You weel not see us, but we weel be watching you."

Before I could reply, the French robot hung up. I dropped the receiver into my lap, leaned my head against the wall, and closed my eyes. "Now I know where to take the ransom. If only I had some ransom to take."

"So it didn't turn out right?" Hank spoke from in front of me, disappointment in his voice. I opened my eyes.

"What?"

"The last frog."

"Where?" I looked around without seeing a frog.

"Here." Hank reached down a hand and pulled me

to my feet. The receiver fell off my lap with a thud, and he picked it up and replaced it on the phone. Then he pointed across the room toward one of the doors onto the deck.

Next to the door was a small table which held a vintage table lamp from Denmark. In front of the lamp hunkered a frog.

I crossed the room and stared down at it. I'd only seen the real Egyptian frog once, but this one looked just as plastic, just as mottled. In the morning light it appeared a bit lighter in color than I remembered the other one to be, but without a side by side comparison I was sure no one could tell. I picked up the object, and it was almost as heavy as the original.

"Wow," I breathed. "You did it." I looked up at him over the frog. He was beaming.

"Oh, good, you like it."

"I do," I nodded. "It's just as ugly as the other one."

He laughed. "I'll take that as a compliment. I knew at least you liked the clay part."

"Yes? How did you know that?"

He stared at me. "You said so."

I stared back. "I did?"

"Don't you remember? I was still working on mixing colors, before I started making frog bodies. I rolled out this sheet of clay, and asked you if it looked right. And you lifted your face off the table and said it was perfect."

I shook my head. "I don't remember a thing. I bet I put my face right back on the table, didn't I?"

"True. But your eyes were open and you were talking."

"Doesn't mean a thing," I assured him. "When we were kids, my cousin thought it was hilarious to wake me up in the middle of the night and ask me questions. There was no telling what I would say, and I never remembered it in the morning."

"If you never remembered, how do you know she did that?"

I studied the frog a bit longer, then set it back on the table. "Because she did it at a slumber party when we were in junior high, and I thought I'd never live down the embarrassment."

"Cousins," he growled.

"True. Though you definitely win with yours. Mine has never tried to murder me."

"There is that," he conceded. "All right, given that you don't remember approving the clay, I venture to guess you don't remember about the paint either?"

"Paint? What paint?"

"I found some little bottles of paint in the box with the clay," he said, "and one of them was gold. So once I finally had a workable frog body, I painted it gold before I covered it with the clay."

"You did? You're a genius!"

"Yeah, seemed like a good idea. If I were a kidnapper, I'd chip off some of the clay to make sure I'd been given the real thing for the ransom."

"Except that trying to ransom two kidnapped dogs with a fake ancient Egyptian frog made of aluminum foil and polymer clay is such a weird thing to do you might just assume it has to be the real thing."

"In that case, we're needlessly out half a bottle of gold paint."

"Well worth it," I assured him.

He nodded. "Come along. Let's have breakfast. I've always made it a rule never to use fake artifacts to ransom kidnapped dogs from French robots on an empty stomach."

19

We hadn't even left the garage before things started going wrong.

"I don't understand it," Hank said, trying once more to put the car key into the ignition.

"Maybe you're nervous and your hands are shaking?" I suggested.

"I may be a bit nervous, I've never been involved in a ransom drop before," he admitted, "but my hands are not shaking." He turned the key over and tried again. No dice. I could feel my internal clock ticking. We needed to be on our way if we were to arrive at the old barn at the designated time.

Realization dawned. "Hank, were the keys hanging on the right or left side of the rack?" I asked.

He shook his head. "Don't remember. I just grabbed them."

"I bet you grabbed Bob's keys." I felt a pang of mingled guilt (that I hadn't driven his car yet as I'd promised) and longing (wishing that he were here holding my hand).

Hank opened the car door. "I'll go get the others."

"No, let's just switch cars. It'll be quicker." I reached across with my left hand and pulled up the latch for my door. Bob's car sat patiently on the other side of the roomy garage. We scrambled into it.

Now the key was perfectly willing to cooperate. It turned sweetly in the ignition and the engine sprang to life. My shoulders went down a tiny notch. Hank shifted into reverse, turned to look over his shoulder and backed out of the garage. Pausing, he said, "Where is the remote control?"

"In the other car," I admitted. "I never got one for Bob's car. Never mind, just leave it open."

But he was already out of the car and hurrying back to the garage. He grabbed the remote off the visor in my car and trotted back, shooting the door shut as he came. As he slid his tall bulk into the driver's seat he tossed the device onto my lap, and I put it into the glove box.

My hands were shaking.

Hank made a three-point turn in front of the garage with a minimum of fuss. In an effort to pretend this was an ordinary errand, I said, "Lucky for me you know how to drive a stick shift. Not everyone bothers to learn these days."

"My dad had a horrible old sports car, an Austin Healy Sprite," he said, "and I learned on that." He put the car in first and started down the drive.

"Why was it horrible? I remember those, they were cute." Good, good, said the encouraging voice in my head. You're conversing like a normal human be-

154

ing. I found that my left hand had a death grip on the bundle in my lap that contained the fake Egyptian frog. I opened the glove box and thrust it inside next to the remote.

"Oh, it was cute, all right, but things were always going wrong with it. Pieces would fall off in the middle of the road as you were driving along. I got good at turning around because I was always having to double back to retrieve bits of it. Also, it had no heat, and—"

He broke off. A blue sedan had pulled off the road into the drive and blocked our way. It moved forward to a few feet in front of us and stopped. The driver's door opened. My heart revved and began to hammer. I held my breath, expecting a silver robot wearing a beret to emerge.

Instead, Mrs. Johnson appeared, holding Prince Henri. She hurried to my side of the car. I rolled down the window.

"Louisa," she said, "I must talk to you."

"I have an appointment—" I began.

Her face was gray under her makeup, as though she were about to have a heart attack. She appeared not to have heard what I'd said.

"When I was here yesterday and your friend told us about the old man who had the stroke, I was...horrified. You see, as I was leaving the flea market, I walked past a car with a little poodle in it, and the day had gotten very hot, and the poor thing was gasping. I looked around to see if anyone was coming to let it out, and no one was in sight. I've never cared much for dogs, but I couldn't just let it die, could

155

I? And in such a horrible way?" she demanded. The fluffy dog in her arms peered up at her face.

"Of course not," I said. "But I must—"

"I tried the car door and it was unlocked. I was simply going to roll down the windows and then wait to make sure the creature did not jump out. I planned to give the owner a piece of my mind. But then...then I picked up the little thing, and—and something happened." She looked down at the dog in her arms, then back at me. "He peered up at me with those bright eyes, and he licked my wrist just once, and I...we connected."

"Yes, but—"

"I felt so angry that anyone could be so stupid as to leave him in the car like that where he could die. So I—" she gave a little gulp, "I took him. I stole him. I, who have never stolen anything in my life, stole someone's dog." Her arms tightened around Prince Henri.

Mrs. Johnson had *stolen* Prince Henri? "Anyone would have done the same."

She glared. "I am not 'anyone,'" she snapped. "I am the president of the Methodist Women's Caucus and a member of the Library Board. Not to mention the mother of the police chief."

"Yes, of course. But we have to—"

"I told myself I was following the greater good, and that I was justified. And every day Prince Henri has been with me, I love him more. I don't know how I can bear to give him up."

"You saved his life. Now we really—""

"Be that as it may, your friend indicated that the

156

loss of his dog has impeded the man's recovery. I cannot have that on my conscience. And the fact remains that I stole him. He isn't mine, no matter how much I love him. You must take Prince Henri back for me."

"What? Me? No, I'm sorry, I have an important, um, meeting in a few minutes and—"

"You must," she said, summoning the imperious resonance with which I am sure she ruled the Methodist Women's Caucus and the Library Board. "I am too ashamed to go, and..." her face crumpled as she fought tears, "...and giving him back is more than I can bear. You must."

She bent her face to the little dog, took a couple of long breaths, then pushed him into my window. I grabbed at him with my left hand. She turned, stumbling back to her car as though her eyes were blinded with tears. The blue sedan backed quickly down the drive, onto the road, and drove away.

Prince Henri licked my chin. "Don't try your tricks on me," I told him gruffly.

"Should I leave him in the house?" Hank asked.

I shook my head. "Put him in the back seat and let's get going," I said, nudging the dog toward Hank. "We'll deal with him later."

Hank boosted the poodle over the seat and put the car in gear. Down the drive, onto the road. I looked around. "Do you think we're really being watched? The robot said we'd be watched the whole time."

"Could be. Or it could be a bluff. It feels like when you're followed by the police on the freeway, though," You're positive you'll make some stupid error and be pulled over any moment."

We rounded the first corner and headed down hill, skirting Quarry Pond. Prince Henri put his front feet between our seats and leaned into the curves. We rode in silence for several minutes until Hank braked to a stop for a red light at Prairie Avenue. A car horn behind us blaring the first notes of "La Cucaracha" made me start and turn around. Dan hopped nimbly down from the driver's seat of his pickup.

"Hey, Louisa! Hey, Hank!" he called, scurrying up and bending down to look in Hank's window.

"Dan," I said. "we're, um, kind of in a hurry."

"I won't keep you," he promised. "Missed you at the park this morning. Hey, is that Mrs. Johnson's poodle? How come you've got him? Where's Emily Ann and Jack?"

"Long story, sir," Hank drawled. I didn't know how he could remember when to use his fake accent, but so far the only time I'd heard him slip up was when he'd been bashed on the head. "I do need to get Mrs. McGuire to her appointment."

A short whoop of police siren made us all jump. A cruiser nosed around from behind Dan's pickup and slid to a stop beside him. The morning sun flashed on the glass as the passenger door window slid silently down. I felt sweat pop out on my forehead as panic ran through me.

"Didn't your kindergarten teachers tell you that the green light means go?" called Ed from his seat behind the wheel. "You people are blocking traffic."

Dan straightened and did a slow turn, looking in

all directions, then said, "What traffic?"

"If you all stay here much longer I'm going to haul you in for vagrancy. Why don't you take this conversation down to the Bluebird? I'm heading that way myself."

If French Robot really was watching, if it saw us talking to the police, it might think I was telling Ed about the dogs being kidnapped. Something terrible could happen to Emily Ann and Jack. My seatbelt felt like a strait jacket.

"We've got to get out of here," I muttered to Hank from between clenched teeth.

"I'm taking Mrs. McGuire to an appointment," Hank said. "In fact, we're running late. We really need to go."

Ed grinned. "How about a police escort? I could turn on the siren and wake everybody up." His expression was hopeful.

"No!" It came out as a shout, and all three men stared at me. Prince Henri barked twice. "Um, no, thanks." I willed my voice to sound normal. "We just need to get going. See you later."

Hank took his cue and put the car in gear, sliding across the intersection as the light turned yellow once more. As he accelerated he glanced in the rearview mirror.

"Ed's not following us, is he?" I asked anxiously, turning my head to look over my shoulder. My view was blocked by Prince Henri, who slurped my glasses. "Ugh. Go lay down, you poodle."

"No, Dan's leaning in the window of the police

car," Hank said. "He looks good for a long conversation." His eyes moved once more to the mirror, then back to the road in front of us. "Now another car has turned the corner and stopped in the other lane and they're all talking."

I breathed steam on my glasses, wiped them on my shirttail, and looked back. "Oh, that's the mayor, Elaine. They could be all morning."

"Good, then they won't be coming after us. I do suggest that if you should ever decide to rob a bank, that you do it in some other town. If you tried it here you'd have an entire entourage complete with police escort to help you."

20

"Turn in there," I instructed, pointing. Hank put on the turn signal, then entered a neighborhood of aging ranch houses. The previous fall Kay and I had reached the old barn that was today's destination via a barely perceptible track that ran behind these houses, off on the west side of the neighborhood. I closed my eyes, trying to remember the sequence of turns. "I think we go right at the first street, and then right again."

Hank made the turns. Nothing looked familiar. I peered at each house as we drove by. "Oh no," I said, "I don't recognize anything. I thought the turn was somewhere along here, but I don't see it." Unwanted tears filled my vision. Would I ever see my dogs again?

"Don't worry, we'll ask someone," Hank said.

"Who? No one's around."

"I'll knock on someone's door."

"They'll think you're insane."

"Not asking would be more insane," he said calmly. "Let's look a bit more, and then if we can't find the turn, we'll stop and ask someone."

We continued to cruise slowly, turning as each street curved into another. I had been lost on foot in this neighborhood once in pouring rain, and I knew how quickly every house started to look like every other. At least this time I was in a car, and dry.

"Maybe they'll know," Hank said. I looked in the direction he was pointing, and saw several tanned, burly young men unloading lumber from a pickup truck. Hank pulled up beside them and called out, "Excuse me, could I ask you for directions?"

They all looked at us, then one flicked the cigarette he was holding into the gutter and stepped over to the car. "Whacha lookin' for?"

"We need to find the road or track to an old barn that's off over that way." Hank waved his arm in the general direction we wanted to go. "I understand you can get there from this neighborhood somewhere."

The guy frowned, chewing on his lower lip. "Never heard of nothin' like that," he said, shaking his head. "Course, I don't live around here. Sorry, can't help you."

"What about your friends, might one of them know?" Hank persisted.

"Nah, we all came over from High Cross to help Norbert's mom build a deck. She just bought this place so no use askin' her neither. Sorry."

He turned and went back to the pickup as Hank said, "Thanks anyway, then." He gave no sign of having heard.

"Let's go," I said. "Maybe someone else will be

around."

Hank put the car in gear and pulled away. "I'm starting to seriously doubt that the dognappers are actually keeping us in view. I don't see how they could be here without us seeing them."

I looked at my watch. We were already a few minutes late for the ransom drop. "I wish they were here," I said crossly. "We could ask *them* where the hell we're supposed to go."

Hank rounded another curve. Ahead we saw someone in a driveway, picking up a newspaper, the shape a black silhouette against the morning sun that was now in our eyes. Hank speeded up a bit and pulled to the curb by the drive. This time our quarry was on my side of the car, and up close proved to be a small old lady in a quilted bathrobe.

I rolled down my window and called, "Excuse me, ma'am..."

She looked up, peering at us through large, lavender framed glasses. "What? Did you say something?"

"I'm looking for a road over to—"

"What's that?"

"Deaf," Hank murmured, and got out. He walked around to my side of the car and said clearly, "Good morning, ma'am. I'm wondering if you could give us directions—"

"Did you come about the car?" she asked, turning her head to look back and forth between Hank and me.

"Car?" I said. "No, we—"

"I wasn't expecting you till later. I haven't had

163

breakfast yet. Have you had breakfast? Why don't you come on in and I'll make you something."

Saints preserve us, said an impatient voice in my head.

"It won't take but a minute, and then you can look at the car. I've got some sausage, I can make you some sausage gravy. And biscuits. Though I may be out of Bisquick, but if I am you can run to the store while I start the sausage cooking."

How about baking yeast bread from scratch, growled the impatient voice.

"Y'all come on in, and let me get dressed, and then—"

Hank had been trying to speak but couldn't stop the spate of words. I pushed my face out the window and said loudly, "No!" This created a small silence, and I quickly pressed my advantage. "No, we didn't come about a car. We need to know—"

"Oh, it's a good car," she assured me. "It was my husband's and he can't hardly drive anymore and he just finally got tired of paying the insurance on it."

Maybe we could use it to run over her, said the resourceful voice.

"He took real good care of it. Your son will like it. Come on in and let me get your breakfast started. You want some eggs with your biscuits? The coffee's already made. I made it first thing when I got up. I been keeping it hot till you all got here to look at the car. You can just park right there. You won't be in the way. Well, I suppose if you want to drive the car before you buy it, you might have to move yours so you can get it out. Oh, look at that, you've got a little poodle. Did you want to bring it in too? I guess that would be okay. We used to have a cat, but—"

"No, we can't," I said loudly and firmly. "This dog is vicious. He bites. We do not want your car. Do you know how we can get to an old barn off to the west of here?"

Hank followed up quickly with, "That's right, we just need directions. But if you don't know, we'll just keep looking, so thanks."

"Oh, that place. Lordy, I don't know why you'd want to go over there for. They keep talking about building more houses but so far it's just been talk. The road's pretty overgrown though. It's over on the next street. Runs between Mary Jacobs' house and the place where they had that fire last month. Everybody got out but the boy had some burns I think, and the insurance is taking their own sweet time paying up. Now Mary, she's really had a time of it. After her husband ran off with that woman from the Texaco, her daughter and her boyfriend moved in, and—"

I bit down hard on my lip to keep from screaming. Stay calm, I told myself, she's just a poor old lady who likes to talk. She's a raving maniac, said the uncharitable voice in my head. Let's get out of here. Unless you think Prince Henri really would bite her.

"We must go," I said.

Hank took his cue. He reached out and took the old lady's hand, giving it a gentle shake. "Thank you so much, ma'am," he drawled. "You've been a huge help. Good luck with the car." He released her hand

and hurried back around the car, sliding inside and starting the engine in one movement. As we sped down the block, I looked back and saw that she was still talking.

"Good lord," I breathed. "I don't even know the woman and I want to kill her. Imagine how her friends and family must feel."

"Louisa!" Hank rolled his eyes at me in mock horror. "How can you say such a thing about a sweet old lady who wants to feed us sausage gravy?"

"Ick," I said. "And first you were going to have to do her grocery shopping for her. At least we might have an idea which street to try. Turn here and let's look again."

The clue of the burned house proved to be what we needed. We'd driven by it earlier, and I realized I'd looked at the scorched shell and missed the turnoff. We took it now, bouncing along the rutted track, over patches of green weeds that had grown luxuriant with spring rain and sun.

21

"Drive faster," I commanded. My right foot was jammed against the floor of the car, as though I could accelerate from the passenger's seat.

"Can't," Hank said. "I'm already speeding, and it would be just our luck to get stopped by your cop friend. He might not give you a ticket, but I'm sure he'd give me one, and I'd rather not have to show my driver's license."

"Oh, yes he would give me a ticket," I said. "He gave Kay one for littering once, and she's his girlfriend. Though she didn't speak to him for months after that."

Prince Henri gave a short bark.

"Did he just pick up on the word 'speak' in that sentence?" Hank asked, glancing in the mirror at the poodle, who barked again.

"I'd say yes," I answered. "I wonder if Mrs. Johnson taught him to do that, or his original owner." I knew I was babbling nonsense, but my brain felt like a flea, unable to land for more than a moment on any thought. I twisted in my seatbelt to look in the back seat. Prince Henri wagged at me, bounced first to one window and then the other, then down onto the floor. He scratched at something under my seat. I tried to see what he was doing but couldn't turn far enough. "He's found a ball or something stuck under my seat. Must have left it in here after we went to the dog park." I faced forward again. "Drive faster. What if Emily Ann and Jack aren't at the house?"

"They will be," Hank said reassuringly. "Whoever took them, the dogs are only a means to an end for them. They'll want to get them off their hands as soon as they can. Especially if it's my cousin Bernard."

"I still can't believe the fake frog will fool them," I worried, then thought I'd been tactless. "Even though you did an amazing job with it."

"All we need right now is to fool them long enough to get your dogs back." Hank made the turn onto my road, and we started up the hill.

Behind us, I heard Prince Henri making play growls at his toy. My flea brain wondered what had gotten left in Bob's car. He was usually so meticulous about keeping it clean, but maybe in his hurry to leave for California he'd forgotten something. Then, over the noise of the engine, I heard something ripping from behind me. I twisted around in my seat again, but the seatbelt still wouldn't let me see the floor.

"Whatever you're tearing up, stop it," I said crossly. "Come on, Prince, leave it."

At the sound of his name, the fluffy little dog jumped back onto the seat. He held a wad of wrinkled tissue paper between his front teeth. His bright little brown eyes sparkled as he peered at me, then he gave his prize a sharp shake.

"Oh, good, you've broken its neck," I told him. "What a brave dog you are. What the heck did Bob leave in the car?" Prince Henri didn't answer. He dropped the paper on the seat and dove back onto the floor.

"Damn!" Hank exclaimed loudly. I jumped. "I don't think I like this."

"What?"

"That car behind us. It's been there too long and now it's too close."

I raised my eyes to look out the back window. A large, muscular-looking gray sedan was so near that all I could see was an expanse of hood and the smoked glass of the windshield. Hank accelerated as we started into the right-hand curve that climbed around the rim of the old quarry.

I turned back around in my seat, feeling suddenly claustrophobic in the embrace of the seatbelt. Then a loud thump jolted the small car. "What the—" I started.

"They're ramming us," Hank said, through gritted teeth. "Hold on."

He gripped the steering wheel so tightly that his knuckles stood out in white knobs. Another jolt and thud. Another. We kept climbing the hill. I looked over my shoulder once more and felt a thrill of relief when I saw the other car had dropped back a bit. But then it surged forward and around and was driving alongside.

169

Crowded nearer, and nearer still. Hank flinched and made a wordless exclamation as the other car turned into ours.

And then we were curving out into the air and flying over the quarry. Time ceased to exist. Our downward flight took either forever or an instant. The only view was the surface of the water, closer, closer, there —and a shuddering jolt. The only sound was a roar of adrenaline surging into my blood. My seatbelt dug into my chest as the nose of the car sank.

22

I tried my best to scream, but all that emerged was a piteous whimper. A similar whimper echoed from the back seat. The car hung suspended on the surface of the water for one heartbeat, two, then tilted more sharply and sank.

Hank scrabbled at his door, but I was frozen into immobility. Was he going to leave me in here? But his fingers found the window knob rather than the latch. He started furiously to roll down the window, but had only opened it two or three inches before we were under water, and the lever would no longer turn. Water ran in as we sank.

Another whimper escaped me. Hank reached over and gripped my left wrist. "Louisa," his voice was a command, "we will get out of here, do you understand? I will not let you drown."

I turned my head to look at him. He appeared so absolutely sure, his blue eyes looking into mine were so steady, that I felt some of my panic roll away. I gave a little nod.

"Can you swim?" he asked.

"I—I'm better at floating." My voice came out in a croak. "I don't like water in my nose."

His smile flashed in the dim light that wavered through the water that now surrounded us. "Floating is all you need. The water pressure on the door means we can't open it or roll down the window any further. But when enough water gets inside, the pressure will equalize and we can open the doors. Do you see?"

I nodded. Water flowed in through the gap in his window. My toes felt it through my shoes. The liquid cold crept toward my ankles.

"It's going to take several minutes for enough water to get in. Leave your seatbelt fastened for now."

I nodded.

"We'll take several deep breaths just before the water gets over our heads, then one last really deep one. Okay? Then you'll hold your nose...can you do that with your right hand? No, the cast won't let you. Okay, hold your nose with your left. I'll open your seatbelt for you. If you can reach the door latch with your right hand, do it and get out. And as soon as I can open my door, I'll get out and swim over to your side and make sure you're out. Then you'll float to the surface."

More water rushed in, nearly to my knees, snaking higher.

"Wh-wh-what about the dog?" My teeth were chattering and I shivered.

"Not to worry. I'll bring him. He'll just have to hold his breath too."

172

The front of the car gave another jolt, softened this time by the water, as it came to rest on the bottom of the quarry pond. Silty mud bloomed up into the clear water. And something rolled against my ankle.

I gave a little shriek and lifted my feet off the floor. Hank started. "What? What is it?"

"S-something's down there, something heavy. It hit my foot when the car bumped down. Oh god, is it a fish or a turtle?" Normally I had nothing against fish or turtles, but I was not in the mood to become better acquainted with one right now.

"Let me check." Hank unfastened his seat belt and leaned toward me, reaching down. He felt around on the floor.

"Here we go," he said, leaning a little more, his ear brushing the surface of the rising water. He stretched out his fingers. "Got it."

He sat back up, holding up a soggy something. A fist sized lump wrapped in disintegrating tissue paper. My eyes widened.

"Th-that's it!"

"What?"

"The Egyptian frog!"

"What!"

He goggled at the bedraggled object in his hand. I reached over and began tearing at the paper. Prince Henri snaked between the seats and into my lap, reaching for the frog with his sharp little teeth.

"No!" we cried in unison. The dog pulled back, looking from me to Hank and back. Hank picked him up one handed and held him against his chest, and I finished pulling off the soggy tissue. I took the frog from Hank, holding it out so we could both look at it.

In the watery light the object in my hand was as ugly as ever, the mottled yellow and green of its covering taking on a sickly hue. A surge of red anger surged over me, and I thrust the thing back toward Hank.

"Here," I choked out.

"What's wrong?" he asked, taking the frog. Prince Henri stretched out his nose to sniff at it.

An incredulous laugh escaped me. I felt water rising higher on my legs. "What's wrong? We're at the bottom of a pond in a leaky tin can because of this thing. I really don't want to die because of a stupid frog!"

"You won't." He appeared as positive as ever. "We'll be back on land in a few minutes. And we're not here because of the frog. We're here because of the greed of some very nasty people. I for one do not intend to die to gratify them."

Four or five large gray fish swam past the windshield. The rising water came in steadily, cold, like utter darkness creeping up my body.

"Okay," I said. "Let's get out of here."

His smile flashed again. "Brilliant. Let me put the frog—here, take the dog, would you?" He started to hold Prince Henri toward me, but the poodle wiggled out of his hand and into the back seat, then all the way to the back of the car.

"Prince, here!" I called. He barked once but didn't come.

"Damn," Hank said. He stuffed the Egyptian frog

174

into the front of his shirt. "All right, I'll unlock the back hatch and get him before I swim up after you. Don't worry about him." He took the key out of the ignition and tucked it into his shirt pocket.

"Can—can dogs hold their breath?" I asked.

"Sure they can." He sounded like he knew this for a fact. How could he be so calm? "Okay, we're going to start our deep breaths. Just a few more minutes and you'll be out on dry land." He reached over and took my left hand in a firm grip.

Taking a deep breath when you are trapped under twenty feet of water in a groaning little car is not an easy thing to do. But I tried. The first attempt was more of a gasp, but then I caught the rhythm of Hank's breathing and followed that. As I did, Bob's face swam before me, smiling encouragement, then I saw Kay, and Jack and Emily Ann. As the water surged up to my chest, my neck, I thought of a day last fall when Bob and I had taken the dogs for a walk along the creek behind his house, and how the sun had slanted through the branches of the trees and turned the falling leaves into pure gold. A perfect day, and it had been mine.

Hank let go of my hand, I took one more deep breath and held it. I clamped my nose shut just as the water rose over my face. Panic rattled through me as I felt the coldness close over my head.

Screaming now would definitely be counterproductive.

Hank reached down and clicked open my seatbelt. I floated over my seat, my head bumping against the

175

ceiling of the car. The world turned in slow motion.

I forced my eyes to stay open. Hank turned away from me and pulled his door latch, shoving with his shoulder. It didn't budge. He tried again. Nothing. He pulled back, then rammed his body once more against the door, and tumbled over as it gave way.

Hank might have been an oversized figure on land, but in the water he was lithe as an eel. He slithered out of the car and swam out of sight. Oh god, what if he leaves me here? said a stricken voice in my head. I tried to grasp the door latch with the fingers of my right hand, but the cast wouldn't let me, and the movement caused me to float away from the door. I was afraid to let go of my nose, knowing how the water would run down my throat. The air in my lungs pressed my head against the roof.

Then movement rippled outside my window, and Hank pulled the door open. I was out of the car. Rising, rising, floating upward toward shimmering light.

23

I collapsed on the rocky bank, my feet hanging over the water. The feeling of sun on my back and fresh air in my lungs was the most wonderful gift I would ever be given. One more breath, two, then I rolled over and sat up.

Miraculously, my glasses were still clinging to my face. I pulled them off and wiped the water streaming from my hair out of my eyes, then gave the glasses a shake. I had nothing dry to wipe them with, so I used my fingers and put them back on. A bit fuzzy, but they would clear in a minute.

I scanned the surface of the pond. No sign of Hank and Prince Henri. I frowned and bit the inside of my lip. I rose onto my knees to hold my cast up to let the water drain from it.

The voices in my head recovered from their fear-induced silence. "That was the scariest thing ever," said the fatuous one. "Well, duh," muttered the sarcastic. "I don't know, having a gun pointed at you by a crazy person wasn't too much fun either," pointed out the perfectionist. "And Hank kept us from being too scared. Now, if he hadn't been with us..."

The voice trailed off. Where was Hank? And that stupid poodle? If something happened to him because of the dog—

Movement on the surface of the water riveted my attention. Prince Henri's head popped out of the water, his curls plastered to his skull. He was facing away from me and started to swim. He wouldn't be able to climb out of the water on the side where he was headed.

"Prince!" I called. "Here, boy!"

He slewed around at my call. As soon as I saw he was moving toward me I took my eyes off him and began anxiously scanning the pond again. Where the hell was Hank? Seconds ticked by, or minutes or hours, with no sign of him.

"Why the hell didn't you learn to swim better when you were a kid?" said the accusing voice in my head. "Don't give me that old 'I don't like water in my nose' excuse. If Hank drowns it's going to be your fault."

Where was Kay when I needed her? She was the one who swam like a fish, who had the junior lifesaving badge when she was twelve. I had been content to paddle on the surface; my amply-padded frame had plenty of built-in buoyancy. Swimming was just a way to cool off on a hot day.

Well, today was hot. My soaked clothing clung to me in a clammy embrace. But the chill I felt waiting for Hank came solely from inside.

From the corner of my eye I saw Prince Henri

climb out of the water several yards to my right. He gave a snort and a mighty shake. Drops of water hit me and spangled the surface of the pond. I took a deep breath and stumbled onto my feet. I didn't know what I could do, but I had to get back in that water and see if I could help Hank.

He burst out of the water just then, very much like the whales I'd seen breaching off Puget Sound. A powerful surge up into the air, then a fall back into the water.

"Hank!" I yelled. "Hank, are you okay?"

He waved a hand at me, then turned onto his back to float. I could see him inhale a great lungful of air and let it out, then another, before he flipped over and began to stroke for shore. He swam towards me and crawled out, sinking onto the grass just as I had. That was when I noticed he was no longer wearing a shirt. No wonder he was such a good swimmer; his musculature was impressive.

"I was just getting ready to look for you," I told him, pleased at my matter-of-fact tone. I sank onto the grass next to him.

He nodded and rolled over onto his back. His eyes were closed. After a moment he said, "I really love the sun."

"Me too. And air. I really love air."

"Oh yeah."

"You okay?"

He sat up. Water streamed from his hair and ran in rivulets over his face and shoulders. He took another deep breath and let it out slowly. "I am, no thanks

179

to that benighted poodle. Where is the beast?" He looked around and spotted Prince Henri several feet away, sitting where he'd emerged from the pond.

"What happened?"

"I thought at first he was panicked in the water. When I got the back of the car open he swam away from me, back to the rear seat again. The ruddy thing must have been an otter in his last life. Then he swam out the passenger door and followed you up."

"So what happened to your shirt?"

"One of my blasted sleeve buttons got caught on something. I couldn't slide it out, so I finally ripped the buttons off the front and got out of the shirt. I never knew how hard it is to tear cloth when it's wet."

"Where's the Egyptian frog? You put it down the front of your shirt."

He tossed it onto my lap from the fist he'd been clutching it with. "Here you go. Hang onto it, will you?"

My linen pants had roomy pockets. I stuffed the frog into the left one.

A few beats of silence went by before I said, "So now what? Should we hike up to the road and flag somebody down? We need to tell Ed what happened right away."

"I have a better idea," Hank said. His voice was grim.

"Yeah? What?"

"I am going to find my bloody cousin Bernard and kill him."

24

A gray sedan with dark tinted windows loomed in my driveway by the path to the front door. I peered down at it through a screen of bushes, then sank onto the ground.

"Ouch!" A sharp pain in my butt indicated that a stiff branch objected to my sitting on it. I scooted a bit to the left, hoping that the plant I was getting near was not the poison ivy it appeared to be. The Egyptian frog poked into my hip through my pocket and I squirmed.

"What?" whispered Hank, sparing me a glance over his shoulder.

"Nothing. I'm fine," I hissed back. "Relatively fine. Is that the car I think it is?"

He turned back to look through the bushes again. "Looks like it. Check out the marks on the front bumper. I think they match the paint of a certain small car now sitting at the bottom of Quarry Pond."

"That's good—physical evidence." Oh, so now you're a crime scene investigator? mocked the sarcastic voice in my head. I ignored it. "But what do we do now? I'm thirsty, you're sunburned, we need to get to a phone, and my house has been invaded." I was not proud of the whiney quality to my voice. Prince Henri came over from the stump he'd been inspecting with his nose. I picked him up and hugged his little poodle body to me. This must be why people kept small dogs, they were like a child's comfort blanket—soft and warm and easily portable.

"Shh! Someone's coming out."

Hastily I set the dog down and rocked onto my knees, pulling apart some branches so I could see. Hank's cousin Bernard bustled out the door, carrying a well-stuffed backpack and the canvas briefcase I'd seen in Hank's room. He put them in the back seat of the car and returned to the house.

"I bet he's clearing out all my things," Hank murmured. "Erasing any evidence I've been here. Wonder if he'll wipe my fingerprints off everything."

"But a lot of people know you're here," I objected. "My cousin, people at the dog park, Mrs. Johnson—"

"Yes, but none of them know my real identity. And no one at home knew where I was going. I just grabbed my passport and as much cash as I could lay my hands on and hared off after Bernard."

"Good thing you're not really dead," I said.

"Yeah. Listen, I bet my clothes are in that bag. I'm going to see if I can get it."

Before I could utter any objections, he slithered away through the brush and made a crouching run across to the car. Prince Henri bounced behind him. A few more silent steps and he had the back door open, then he was returning, clutching the backpack to his chest, poodle at his heels. His breathing was hardly faster than when he left.

"Got it." He zipped open the top. "Bingo." A dark blue tee shirt was on top of the mess stuffed into the bag. Hank pulled it out and put it on. "That's better. It's always easier to confront Bernard when one is clothed."

"What do you mean?"

"There are two of us and only one of him, and he's actually a sniveling coward. We can overpower him and find out what's going on."

"And call Ed."

"Absolutely. This is my chance to get Bernard out of my hair for a good long time. I imagine attempted murder of two people will carry a stiff sentence, even here in the wilderness."

"It wouldn't look like such a wilderness if you had ever mowed the grass."

"Indeed. Sorry about that. I've been a rotten gardener, haven't I?" His accent was at its most British.

"Rotten," I agreed. "What's the plan?"

"I wonder if the back door is locked?"

"I usually lock it when I leave the house, but I don't know if I did today. I was only thinking about Jack and Emily Ann. Who clearly are not here," I added.

"I know, they'd have found you by now."

I nodded, unable to speak.

"All right. Let's do it." He rose easily to his feet,

and held a hand down to me. I grasped it and he pulled me up. "Ready? Here we go."

I felt like we were two characters in an old war movie, about to try our daring escape from the prison camp. I followed my captain out of the brush. The glass walls of the house were the guard tower, but no shots rang out as we walked rapidly to the front door, which proved not only to be unlocked, but also open a couple of inches. Hank eased it open and we stepped into the entry.

Silence. Then a creaking floorboard upstairs told me where Bernard was. The creak was followed by a humming drone. This settled into a tune, and after a few bars I recognized the song about the teddy bears having a picnic. My spine stiffened. It was bad enough that he had tried to kill us, but afterward to be humming about a picnic was outrageous.

Prince Henri followed us into the house. When he heard the humming his ears cocked forward and he dashed past Hank, trotting up the stairs. Hank made a grab for him but missed. Upstairs, the humming stopped.

"Good lord, not another mutt," I heard Bernard exclaim. "How many creatures did that woman have? And where did you come from? Never mind, out you go."

Hank and I sprang into action, dashing into the guest room and pressing ourselves against the wall beside the door as Bernard's footsteps descended the circular stairs. What if he comes in here? screamed the most easily panicked voice in my head. Shut up, we'll jump him, replied a more stalwart one. The foot-steps passed the open guest room door and out to the front porch.

"Now get out of here," Bernard said, presumably to the dog. Then he shouted, "No! Get away, you little shit! Don't you dare pee on that car!" His footsteps crossed the porch and down the steps.

"Quick, upstairs!" Hank hissed in my ear. We hurried out of the room and up the stairs. Hank looked around, then scurried into the bathroom. I followed, closing the door partway and standing behind it so I could see through the crack into the living room. Hank moved in behind me. I heard Prince Henri yelp, then silence from outside. The door downstairs slammed, and a moment later we heard Bernard's footsteps on the stairs.

"Bloody dog," he growled. "Better not be any more of them."

As if I didn't already have enough to worry about, now I had to fret over what I was going to tell Mrs. Johnson if something happened to Prince Henri.

Bernard moved into my narrow slice of vision. He held a dishtowel, and as we watched he went to the sliding door onto the deck and rubbed the towel over the handle and door jamb. Then he did the same thing to the lamp on the table nearby.

Hank poked my back. I looked over my shoulder, and he pointed to his fingertips. I nodded. Bernard really was trying to wipe out Hank's fingerprints. Fat chance, said the cynic in my head, rather gleefully. Hank has handled nearly everything in this house.

Bernard continued his task, then threw down the towel and walked toward the bathroom where we were hiding. I sucked in my breath. He shoved open the door, which banged into me, but Bernard didn't notice. He walked toward the toilet, unbuckling his belt as he approached. When I heard the zipper, the entire chorus in my head began to clamor. No! Stop! Why did we have to hide in the bathroom?

I must have made a sound. I think it was something like, "Eeep!" Bernard turned his face in our direction, and saw Hank and me.

He gave a terrified scream and whirled to face us. He put his hands out to ward us off.

His trousers fell down around his ankles, revealing white briefs printed with red lips.

"You're dead!" he yelled. In the small room his voice was deafening. "I saw you go under. You're dead!"

"That's right, Bernard," Hank said. He took two slow, menacing steps toward his cousin. "You did it this time. You not only killed me, but Louisa as well. And now we've come back for you." His voice made me shudder.

"Get away, get away!" Bernard moaned. He took a step to flee, but the pants tripped him and he went sprawling. Hank pounced, pinning his cousin with a knee in the middle of the back. He grabbed Bernard's right wrist and twisted his arm behind him. Bernard howled.

"Shut up, Bernard," Hank growled through clenched teeth, and twisted the arm a little further.

Bernard gave one more yelp and subsided. Hank risked a quick glance over his shoulder. "Louisa, do you have any rope?"

"R-rope?" I gulped, unpleasant possibilities for its use rushing into my mind.

"I want to tie up my dear cousin until the police get here," Hank explained.

"Oh! Um, I might, but I don't know where." I was getting really tired of not knowing where my possessions were located. "But I think I can find a couple of extension cords."

"Brilliant. Would you move one of the dining chairs, the one with the arms, to the middle of the room and get the cords?"

Hank hauled his cousin upright, still with the arm twisted behind. Bernard yelped again. They moved forward and Bernard tripped over the trousers puddled around his ankles.

"My pants," he whined.

"Step out of them," Hank ordered.

I hastened off to find the cords. Fortunately I was able to lay my hands, or rather hand, on them quickly. Hank shoved the shorter man—sans trousers—into the chair.

"Wrap one of them around his body and the back of the chair," Hank told me. "As tight as you can."

I obeyed, but couldn't tie a knot one handed. Hank let go of Bernard and quickly knotted the cord, then grabbed the second one and lashed each wrist to an arm of the chair.

"That's you sorted," Hank said, knotting the second cord. "I'd like another cord for your ankles, but this should suffice until the constabulary can get here." He walked around in front of Bernard and looked down at him with a slight smile. "Bernard, your goose is, at last, cooked."

Bernard's expression was that of a sullen teenager who had been caught smoking in the school bathroom. "Not at all," he returned. "I don't know how you got here, but it's simply your word against mine."

Hank's smile turned into a wolfish grin. "Ah, but it's not. You've left lovely physical evidence this time. Now, before I have Louisa call the police, tell us where her dogs are. That was low, even for you, kidnapping innocent dogs."

"I don't know where they are," Bernard said, glancing at me, then back to Hank.

"Not good enough, cuz. I don't want to have to hurt you, but I'm sure we'll have plenty of time to find out what I want to know before anyone gets here."

"I wouldn't count on that."

The voice coming from the direction of the stairway made the hair on my neck stand at attention. I turned toward it and froze.

Rebecca. Holding a pistol.

Aimed at me.

25

"Who the hell are you?" Hank demanded.

"The one in charge here," she replied coolly. "Untie him." The gun in her hand was perfectly steady.

"She's the person who was supposed to get the Egyptian frog," I said. "Don't let her catch you on a staircase."

The corners of her mouth turned up and she flicked a glance in my direction. Then she said again, "Untie him."

I looked away from her to meet Hank's eyes. He turned to work at the bulky knots holding his cousin to the chair.

"It's about time you got here," Bernard grumbled.

"Shut up. I've been busy."

Hank unwound the long brown cords. As soon as Bernard was free, he pushed up from the chair so fast that it fell over backward. He grabbed the front of Hank's shirt.

"You're going to pay for that," he growled into Hank's face.

Hank's lips curled in amusement. "How? Are you going to try to kill me yet again, dear cousin?"

"Enough," frowned Rebecca. "Where is the frog?"

"Where are my dogs?" I countered, still pinned by the gun to the spot where I'd been standing for what seemed a very long time. The gold frog in my pants pocket grew heavier as I glared at her. I hoped my shirt tail still concealed its bulge.

Rebecca met my eyes and smiled. "Oh, I took care of them."

Cold dread clamped onto the back of my neck. "What have you done?"

"They were fine when I last saw them. Of course, that was when I let them out of the car beside the freeway." Her smile was triumphant.

Hank gasped. "No."

I kept tight control over my face. I didn't want Rebecca to see the sick dread that gripped me. I hoped I would have the chance to make her very, very sorry. I said, "Then I'm happy to tell you that the frog you have gone to so much trouble to obtain was in the car that your partner here shoved into Quarry Pond this morning. Hank and I barely escaped. We certainly weren't worried about a hunk of green plastic."

"What!" The exclamation came from both Bernard and Rebecca. The gun twitched as Rebecca's hand tightened on the grip.

I caught my breath, expecting every breath to be my last. A cross voice in my head complained, Dammit, we already almost drowned today. Getting shot is just not fair! I suddenly wished I had accepted the old lady's offer of breakfast and that I were in her house, gritting my teeth as she prattled.

"Bernard, you ass, you ran them off the road before they made the drop," Rebecca said in an ominously even voice.

"No! No, they were on the way back. I nipped in and picked up the frog and then followed them."

"You picked up a fake," Hank said. "We left the real one in the car."

Bernard gave Hank a head-rattling shake. "Tell me that's a lie," he demanded.

Hank looked down on his cousin as though on a gnat. "Perfectly true," he said. He gave Bernard a sudden shove. Bernard stumbled backward, letting go of Hank's shirt. Rebecca turned on them, and my shoulders went down several inches.

"Stop it! This is no time for horse play. Bernard, can you swim?"

"No."

"Oh, you can too," said Hank.

"No. I haven't for years. You're the one who inherited the estate with the pool." His voice was petulant.

"Shut up, both of you. Louisa, you and his lordship are going to take us to that pond. Is there a road?"

"No," I said quickly, before Hank could answer. A picture of the winding drive to the pond unrolled before my eyes. I hoped Rebecca was not psychic. "You have to hike in—or be driven over the cliff."

"All right, let's go. Bernard, get your pants on."

He looked down at himself, and flushed. Without a word he hurried into the bathroom. He returned, still

191

buckling his belt.

Rebecca gestured with the pistol. "Bernard, you go down the stairs first, then His Grace here. Then Louisa. I will be right behind Louisa with the gun. And if you're thinking about trying anything heroic, keep in mind that Louisa is completely expendable."

As we emerged from the house, Prince Henri jumped down from the hood of Bernard's car and pranced over to us. I gave a little sigh of relief. He seemed none the worse for his encounter with Bernard. Maybe Bernard had been the one yelping earlier.

Hank led the way past the garage, down the hill and through the woods to the pond. When I'd climbed out of the water an hour before, I'd vowed never to go there again. Usually I kept my promises a little longer than this.

A family of ducks floated serenely on the surface of the pond, in the shallows near the edge. As our little parade approached, the mother duck swam toward the far side, followed by her flotilla of six or seven yellow babies. The scene was so peaceful that the sight of Rebecca with her gun became even more surreal.

Prince Henri did not like the ducks. He ran along the shore barking, then launched himself into the water. Without hesitation the mother duck came at him, quacking and flapping her wings. The poodle quickly decided he'd had enough swimming and scrambled back to shore. He gave a mighty shake and Rebecca shrieked when the water hit her. The mother duck and her little family swam away.

"All right, your lordship, into the water." Rebecca gestured with the gun.

"It's too far down," I protested. "He nearly drowned getting out before."

"Louisa, shut up," she snarled. "Go get that damned frog, do you hear me? Or I swear I'll start shooting. First Louisa, and then your cousin, and then that damned poodle."

Hank shrugged, and pulled the blue tee shirt over his head. "I suggest you start with Bernard rather than Louisa," he said calmly, dropping the shirt. The jeans were next, revealing navy blue boxers. Better than tighty-whities with lips on them, muttered a relieved voice in my head. He walked to the edge of the water and waded in. He launched himself into the water with a long shallow dive, swam several strokes, then jackknifed his way under water.

"What do you mean, you're going to shoot me?" Bernard huffed. I could see exactly what he must have looked like as a baby when his will was thwarted.

"Shut up, Bernard," Rebecca snapped. Her eyes were still on the pond, but the gun pointed at me.

"What's with this frog thing, anyway?" I asked. I eased my left hand into the pocket, hoping that wouldn't call attention to the lump there. "I mean, I understand why Bernard here stole it, he wanted to be the duke and he's jealous—"

"He should never have been born!" Bernard burst out. "Everyone knew I was the heir, and then *he* came along."

"Right." I tried to sound soothing. Bernard looked like a time bomb, and I wasn't sure if it would be to my advantage if he were to explode. "You were the heir. But Rebecca, what's with you? My cousin says you're terrific with antiques, yet here you are with a gun in your hand looking for a frog."

"That frog is going to solve a lot of problems for me," she snapped. "And if I don't turn it over to its new owner—who by the way has already given me a lot of money for it—my old problems will be a stroll in the park by comparison."

From the road atop the cliff on the other side of the pond a car horn tapped out "Shave and a haircut." We all looked up. Dan was leaning out of the window of his idling pickup, waving down at us.

Rebecca quickly moved the gun behind her back. "Wave back," she growled at me. I obeyed, wishing I could think of some signal that would alert Dan that I needed help. I thought briefly about flipping him the finger but figured he'd just laugh. He gave one more wave and continued driving down the hill.

A splash from the pond heralded Hank's return to the surface. He was about twelve feet from shore, which I knew was not as far out as the car. He gasped for air as he trod water, splashing rather wildly with his arms.

"Well?" Rebecca called. "Did you find it?"

Hank shook his head. He seemed to have trouble catching his breath. "I don't...think...I can dive...that far," he gasped. "The car is...about...fifty feet...down."

Quarry Pond is about twenty feet deep. Everyone

194

in town knew that—but no one would have told Rebecca or Bernard.

"Try again," Rebecca commanded. Hank shrugged.

"Just...a minute," he wheezed. "I need...to catch my breath."

More splashing. Hank took a number of deep breaths, then finally dove back under the surface.

"You're going to have to send someone down in diving equipment," I said, hoping to convey that I knew what I was talking about. "It's a long way down and they'll have to search inside the car once they get there."

Rebecca scowled at me. "When I want your opinion I'll let you know."

"I'm just telling you, you're wasting your time here." I was pleased at the offhand note I got into my voice.

Before she could reply a car horn tooted once more—this time from the woods behind the pond. Dan's truck came barreling up the track that led from the pond out to the road. Rebecca grabbed my left wrist and pulled me in front of her, jabbing the gun into my ribs.

"You said there was no road into here," she growled in my ear.

"I lied."

"Hey, Louisa!" Dan called, jumping out of the truck, followed by his dog Roxie. And then Jack and Emily Ann boiled out of the truck, racing to me. Without thought I jerked my wrist out of Rebecca's grasp and fell to my knees to be engulfed by wagging, wiggling dogs.

It was heaven.

I hugged both, and snuffled over them, hiding my face in Emily Ann's sleek side. Jack gave me some worried kisses. "It's okay," I whispered. "You're back and we'll get out of this. Everything will be okay."

I looked up at Dan. "Thanks."

He scowled at me. "Louisa McGuire, what the hell is going on? Do you know where I found these two? By. The. Freeway." He waved his arms in fury. "The free-way! I couldn't believe my eyes. I was coming along that stretch by Anderson's farm and saw a car pulling back onto the road from the shoulder, and then I saw two dogs. Son of a bitch has dumped those dogs, I told Roxie. I could just kill people like that. So I pulled over and dang it, it was Jack and Emily Ann."

Rebecca nudged me none too gently with her foot. "Get up."

I stayed where I was a bit longer, savoring the feel of Emily Ann's and Jack's sleek coats, then tottered back to my feet. Dan was still frowning at me, ignoring Rebecca and Bernard. "I'll explain later," I promised. "If you see Ed when you get back to town—"

"He's not going anywhere," Rebecca snapped. That got Dan's attention. I could tell she had the gun out when his eyes widened in alarm.

"What the hell!"

She grabbed my arm again. "Sit down on the ground, old man," she said, "or I shoot Louisa."

His eyes narrowed—whether at the "old man" or the threat to me I wasn't sure—but without a word he sank down and crossed his legs. Jack was delighted to have him on his level and bustled into this suddenly available lap. I heard a splash behind us and looked toward the pond, expecting to see Hank returning. But it was Roxie, who was getting a drink, up to her belly in the pond. When she noticed Dan sitting on the ground she loped over, followed by Prince Henri. In a moment all four dogs swirled around us. Water dripped from Roxie's muzzle.

"God, I hate dogs," Rebecca complained. "Get them out of here!"

"Go play, you guys," I told them, striving for calm. Dan looked around and picked up a stick lying near him on the ground, tossing it in an arc. The four dogs streamed after it. Roxie reached it first, snatched it up, and loped off with the others following her.

Another splash came from the pond. "He's back," Bernard announced as Hank's head surfaced. "Well?" he called.

Hank swam toward us until the water grew too shallow, then stood and waded in. He gasped theatrically for air as he staggered onto the shore. "It's too far down. I can't do it." He leaned over with his hands on his knees, wheezing.

Rebecca's grip on my arm became a vise. "Try again." Her voice was flat and hard. She pointed the gun at Hank. He looked at her and shook his head.

"Makes no difference if you shoot me or I drown. It's just too deep."

No one was paying attention to Dan. I glanced over and saw he had his cell phone out and was dialing. I wrenched my eyes back to Rebecca and said loudly, "It's awful down there, you can't imagine. It's so deep, I thought I'd never make it to the surface. And dark, and murky, and all these plants try to grab you, and huge gray fish with teeth—"

My tone must have reached the dogs, for they all came running. Prince Henri trotted straight to Dan, who muttered into his phone. "Ed? Ed, it's Dan. Come down to the—"

Rebecca gave a shriek. Bernard launched himself forward and grabbed Dan's phone, pivoted, and threw it into the pond. Cricket, I thought. It looked like a move I'd seen in films of cricket games.

The dogs, excited to have a new object to chase, raced to the pond. Prince Henri launched himself into the water, but his fun new toy had disappeared. He swam back, trotted toward us, and shook. Water flew off his curly hair. Rebecca flinched toward me, bumping into my side.

The side with the Egyptian frog in my pocket.

26

Rebecca became very still, a snake coiled and ready to strike. Her slitted eyes bored a hole through me. At last she spoke.

"What is in your pocket, Louisa?"

"N-nothing," I quavered.

"Show me." She dropped my arm and stepped back a pace, the gun steady on my chest. The three men were frozen with identical blank expressions.

Slowly I dug into my pocket with my left hand, my fingers touching the body-warm plastic surface of the artifact. As soon as I handed it to her, it would all be over. I was certain she would shoot us and roll our bodies into the pond, then drive away in Dan's truck. I looked away from the gun, at the still-widening ripples on the surface of the pond.

Taking a deep breath, I pulled the Egyptian frog out of my pocket with a shaky hand, twisted around, and lobbed it toward the water.

My wobbly left-handed throw was a pitiful thing, low-arced and woefully slow. At the same time, it was perfect—for a dog. Prince Henri leapt forward and caught the frog in mid-air in his grinning teeth, and without a pause dashed off with the other three dogs in pursuit.

Rebecca's breath wheezed out of her body in an audible gasp. She stared wide-eyed at the frolicking dogs, who cavorted along the edge of the pond. Roxie made a grab for the frog in Prince Henri's mouth, which the poodle evaded by ducking his head and making a quick turn, which put him in Emily Ann's path. She leapt into the air to avoid him, and landed in front of Jack, who put on his brakes. Prince Henri made an end run around the two of them and put on speed. The others followed. We could have been at the dog park, except that usually no one there was armed.

"Stop them! Make them stop!" Rebecca grabbed my shoulder and shook me so hard my glasses bounced up and down.

"Ow!" I protested. The bridge of my nose is tender. But I did not call to the dogs. Prince Henri finally dropped the heavy frog, which Roxie immediately scooped up. Their merry chase continued, moving toward us, then swinging away around the curve of the pond. They were joyful and carefree, but no joy showed on Rebecca's face. She was flushed, her jaw set in a grimace. And the gun, which for so long had been aimed at me, was now following the path of the dogs.

Prince Henri sped up and bounded in front of Roxie, who braked so hard that she dropped the frog. Jack was in place, ready to take over. He grabbed frog, threw back his head in triumph, then wheeled on his short legs and began to run.

Directly toward me.

Jack is only half retriever, but he is all good boy. To his mind the right thing to do is bring in your toy so it can be thrown again. Only this time, I knew there would be no second throw. The muzzle of Rebecca's gun was tracking Jack. I had no idea what kind of shot she was, but Jack was running in a straight line and getting closer by the second. Cold, brutal fear clutched me and the sounds of the morning faded till I could hear only a kind of buzzing in my head. Everything around me swayed in slow motion, as though I were once more under the surface of the pond.

Rebecca's face changed to a vicious smile, and I felt as much as saw her finger begin to tighten on the trigger.

"No!" As the single word squeezed from my throat, I raised my right arm, encased in its rock-hard fiberglass cast, and brought it down as hard as I could on Rebecca's wrist.

The gun went off in an ear-shattering blast as it tumbled to the ground. Dirt spurted into the air a few feet away. Without pause I brought the cast back up, connecting with Rebecca's chin in a satisfying crunch. She crumpled to the ground beside her gun.

I stared down at her. As I did, Jack arrived at my side, dropped the frog on my foot, and placed himself between me and Rebecca's body.

Jack had saved my life twice. It was nice to be able to return the favor.

A car door slammed. Dan's truck roared to life. I

201

looked away from Rebecca to see Cousin Bernard back it in an arc, then lurch forward onto the track into the wood. He barreled out of sight.

"Uh oh," said Hank drily. "The ship must be sinking. There goes the rat." He stared after the truck, then gave a small sigh. "Too bad we didn't bring the extension cords with us. We should tie her up before she comes around."

"I've got a rope in the..." Dan began. "Oh. Guess that's not much good."

"I'll just bash her again," I offered. I was panting a little, as though I'd been running. I bent down to pat Jack, who wagged and leaned against my leg. I picked up the Egyptian frog. "Or you could hit her with this." I handed the frog to Hank.

"Thanks," he said, taking it from me. "And I think I'll also hang on to this." He picked up the gun and balanced it in his palm.

"Now what?" asked Dan plaintively. The rest of the dogs bounded up. Prince Henri sniffed Rebecca's ear and gave her face a small experimental lick. "Should we hike up to your place? Or maybe I should walk out to the road and try to flag somebody down?"

"Too bad we lost your phone," Hank said. "I could look for it but they usually don't work after getting wet."

"And mine was in my purse for once, so it's in the pond too," I put in. "The place is getting filled up with phones." The banter helped me ignore the woman's body lying at our feet and the nasty little black gun in Hank's hand.

"All right, I'll go," Dan decided. "I can flag somebody down when I get to the road."

"I'd be glad to—" Hank began, but Dan waved him off.

"Nah, I'm more likely to see someone I know," he said. "Just start working on your story. I've got a lot of questions, starting with what Louisa's dogs were doing on the freeway and going right on up to what's the deal with that frog, and when you grew an English accent. Come on, Roxie."

The big brown dog trotted obediently to his side, but they had only gone a few paces when we heard the rumble of an engine approaching through the woods. A police cruiser bounced around a curve into view and rolled into the clearing. Bernard was in the back seat.

"Well done, Dan," I called. "That was really quick."

Ed climbed out. "Louisa McGuire, can't you stay out of trouble for two minutes?" He walked over to us. "Son," he said to Hank, "how about if you hand over the gun and get some pants on."

Hank looked down at himself in surprise. We'd all forgotten he was standing around in wet boxers. "Of course, sir." He gave Ed the gun. "My apologies."

"It's not his," I hastened to explain, "the gun I mean. It was Rebecca—"

"I know whose gun it is," he interrupted. "If you're going to be knocking people out with your cast, Louisa, I suggest you not do it in full view of a public road." He gestured across the pond.

"If you'd gotten here a little earlier she wouldn't have had to hit the woman," Dan huffed. "What kept you?"

"You mean you tracked us here from that split second phone call?" I asked, impressed.

But Ed shook his head. "Dan called me when he found your dogs by the highway. I headed up to your house, but nobody was home when I arrived."

"No, we'd taken a little hike by then," I agreed.

"Louisa told them there was no road to this place," Hank added.

"Remind me never to believe a word you say, Louisa," Ed deadpanned. "Anyway, I decided to go back to town this direction. I was coming down the hill when I saw your little scene by the pond. Good thing I was too far away to be able to really identify the person who hit the shooter and knocked her out. I'd probably have to arrest whoever it was for assault, but I'm sure he or she is long gone by now."

"But it was self-defense!" I cried.

"I've seen crazier things happen in court," he said, "but it won't come to that. I don't believe any witnesses were around, right, boys?" He looked at Dan and Hank, who nodded vigorously.

"I'm pretty sure she tripped on something and fell and knocked herself out," Dan said. "It's a miracle nobody got hurt."

Rebecca groaned and stirred.

"Guess I better get her in the car," Ed said. "Dan, get me the spare cuffs out of the glove box, would you?"

Dan hurried over to the cruiser, Roxie at his heels. As he leaned in the open passenger window, he said

204

something to Bernard, who answered in a sullen tone, but I couldn't make out their words. Rebecca groaned again and opened her eyes.

"All righty, then," Ed said, leaning over to grasp her arm firmly with both hands. He hauled her to her feet.

"Officer, thank god you're here," Rebecca moaned. "This woman attacked me!"

Ed ignored her. "Let's get you squared away with your pal in the car and get you downtown. We've got some paperwork to do so we can lock you up and throw away the key."

Rebecca's look of loathing encompassed both Ed and me.

Dan returned with the handcuffs. Ed deftly fastened them around Rebecca's wrists. She winced. "Looks like you got a little bruise," he commented as he clicked the cuff around the wrist I'd hit with my cast. "We'll have the doc take a look at it."

I hoped it was broken.

Hank spoke up then. "What did my cousin say to you?" he asked Dan.

Dan smiled a little. "He just said he hates frogs."

27

"Do I hear fifty? I have the fifty. Sixty? Seventy-five at the front." The auctioneer's rhythmic chant floated over the crowd. "Who's got the hundred? Thank you, sir."

"Can you believe this?" I said in Kay's ear. "People will buy anything at this auction."

She cocked an eyebrow at me. "Louisa, don't be so modest. It's never been like this before."

The auctioneer's helper hoisted overhead the painting that was the current object of competition. I knew it well, having found it at a garage sale a few weeks earlier—a framed oil painting of a nondescript dog in front of a lovingly-rendered picket fence. The dog might have been a Yorkie or a beagle; but you could practically tell what brand of paint had white-washed those pickets. Possibly worth the two dollars I had paid for it. No art dealer would have been pre-sumptuous enough to price it at the hundred and thirty five it had reached.

"One fifty, do I hear one fifty? Who'll give me the

fifty?" The auctioneer scanned the crowd. "Don't let this original piece get away, ladies and gentlemen...I have one thirty five once, do I have one fifty?" He paused once more, then closed the deal. "One thirty five twice. And sold for one thirty five to the gentleman on the left."

The gentleman on the left, an oversized specimen with brawny arms and a tattoo on the side of his neck depicting an erupting volcano, raised a fist in triumph, then stepped forward to claim his prize. His buddies crowded around to inspect his purchase. The auctioneer began to describe the next piece for sale.

"Come outside," Kay hissed in my ear. "I need some air."

"And I need some sanity," I mouthed back.

I led the way through the crowd, which parted before me almost magically. They don't want to jostle your broken arm, said the optimist in my head. Yeah, or they think you'll bash them with it, retorted the sarcastic one.

"Whew, hot in there," Kay said when we were outside, fanning her face with her hand. I looked back over my shoulder at the huge, light-filled tent that had been erected in the middle of the dog park.

"It's going great though," I said. "We've raised a ton of money."

"I'll say. Thanks to all the publicity. The timing of your escapade was great."

"Right, an idiot mistook me for a crook, I broke my arm, nearly drowned, the dogs were kidnapped, and we were frog-marched at gunpoint up hill and down dale by a woman who turns out to be wanted in five states, so that more people would come to this auction."

She snickered. "Frog marched?"

"Oh, you know what I mean."

"Hey, whatever works," she said, biffing me on the shoulder.

Her cell phone rang. She pulled it out of her pocket, flipped it open, and looked at it. When did people start looking at a phone before saying hello, I wondered. "Hang on, I need to get this," she said, then into the tiny instrument, "Hello? Hey, how are you!"

I strolled a few feet away, enjoying the cool night air. The auction tent had become more and more ovenlike as the evening progressed and people kept arriving. Heaven knew how far away some of them were parked. Kay's voice followed me.

"Yeah, we're all good...I'll let her tell you. Yeah, she's right here, hang on." Kay held out the phone in my direction. "Hey, Louisa, it's Bob, fresh back from the jungle."

I hurried back and grabbed the little instrument. "Hi!"

"Hi yourself." His voice was warm and familiar. I hadn't realized until this moment just how much I'd missed hearing it. "How are you? Seems like a year since I saw you."

"I'm good," I told him, "everything's fine, except for missing you." Kay raised an eyebrow at me. I held my breath, waiting for him to say something about the Egyptian frog.

"We just got out of the jungle today," he said. "I'm in Mexico, on a little plaza in the middle of town. Well, town might be too major. Suffice it to say I can see a goat and a couple of chickens off to my left."

I laughed, partly in relief. He hadn't seen any papers yet. "Sounds bucolic. How did the jungle stuff go?"

His voice lit with excitement. "Great. I can't wait to tell you about it. I'm not too sure how long the phone's battery will last though. Haven't had a chance to charge it yet."

"No problem," I assured him. "We're at the dog park auction anyway. I'll have to go inside in a minute."

"Oh, that's right. I've lost track of the date. Sorry. Are people buying stuff?"

"Anything and everything, we're making a bunch of money."

"That's great. Jack and Emily Ann are okay? And how's the house, did you get unpacked yet?"

"They're both fine, and I'm mostly unpacked. But listen, I think the lawn mower is broken. The damn thing won't start."

"Did you reconnect the spark plug?"

"Did I what?"

"The spark plug. I always disconnect it. A safety thing my dad always made me do."

Lawn mowers had spark plugs? The things you learn on a Saturday night. "Um, no, but I'll try that. Too bad I didn't ask you before you left."

"You should get somebody to mow for you," he

said.

"Yeah, I tried that, but he wasn't very experienced. He couldn't start the mower either. But we'll be fine now I know about the spark plug."

"You're fading," he said. "Gotta go. Damn. I'll call you in a day or two, okay?"

"Okay. I'll have a lot to tell you. Bye. Miss you!"

His phone's battery must have failed. I heard only silence. Shutting the little phone I handed it back to Kay, who said, "Let me guess. He hasn't heard about what you've been up to."

"Evidently not," I agreed. "But at least now I know how to get the lawnmower started."

"Hey, Louisa!" Dan called from the door of the tent. He jigged over to where we stood. "Can you believe this? We've never made this much on the auction before. I bet we can fix the fence *and* run in a water line."

I smiled at his excitement. "You did a great job organizing everything," I told him.

"Aww, shucks," he twinkled. "It weren't nothin', ma'am. Besides, it was the news stories about your activities that got all these people here. I was just talking to a couple that drove down from Iowa." His voice held awe at the thought of such a trek.

Dan doesn't travel much.

I cringed a little at the reference to the news. I was heartily sick of the media, and not a little apprehensive about what Bob was going to say. I hoped I'd be able to break it to him gently before he read about what had happened in some paper. With any luck, the

210

furor would be completely over by the time he got back.

"I think the reporters are done with me," I told Dan. "There are just a lot of dog lovers everywhere, that's all."

Kay blew a raspberry. "Give it up, cuz. Admit you've become a media darling. You and your duke."

"Have you heard from Hank?" Dan asked.

"He called from Cairo yesterday. The golden frog has been decloaked and reunited with its twin."

"And—" Kay put in, "—National Geographic is doing an article on them."

"Louisa's going to be in National Geographic?" Dan asked, his eyes wide.

"But not topless," Kay assured him.

"All right, you guys," I groaned. "We'd better get back inside. We might need to bid on something."

"I don't think I can afford anything at this auction," Kay said.

"Not much left," Dan said. "We'll be wrapping it up soon."

We ooched our way back through the crowd. Three contenders bid briskly for a pair of china dog candlesticks. We had almost reached the front when someone grabbed my arm. "Louisa!" said a woman's voice in my ear.

"Oh, Joan, hello. How nice of you to come," I said. Then I saw that the minister's wife was standing next to Mrs. Johnson, who was holding Prince Henri. "Prince! You're back!"

I had delivered the poodle to Joan the day after

our adventure by the pond so that she could return him to his rightful owner.

"Mr. Bantry is better," Joan explained, "but he'll be going to an assisted living place and he can't have the dog there. So he sent Prince Henri back to stay with Mrs. Johnson."

I scratched the poodle on his fluffy top knot. "I'm so glad you have him back," I told Ed's mother. "I know you missed him."

"Yes," she nodded, "I did." Her eyes were suspiciously bright.

Joan burbled on, "Knowing his dog was safe was what put Mr. Bantry back on the road to recovery. He's so grateful to Mrs. Johnson for rescuing him."

Mrs. Johnson turned pink. She looked at the ground. On stage, the auctioneer finished selling the candlesticks. I looked around to see what was left to sell. Dan was on stage talking into the auctioneer's ear. Then he scanned the crowd in the tent, and pointed in my direction.

"Uh oh," I said. "I think I have to go now."

The auctioneer spoke into his microphone. "Ladies and gentlemen, you all know what a great cause we're supporting here tonight. We have one more item to sell. One more very special item. But before we do that, let's hear from a lady who's one of the dog park's staunchest supporters—Louisa McGuire!"

I tried to get around Mrs. Johnson, but she blocked my way. "Louisa, where do you think you're going?" she demanded.

"Home," I said. "I need to mow the lawn."

She snorted. I had never thought to hear her make such a plebian sound. "Get yourself up on that stage and do your civic duty."

"Yeah!" cheered Joan.

"Why is this my civic duty? They're just putting me on show."

Her expression softened a little at the edges. "People are interested in you, that's all. Simply thank everyone for coming. You don't have to orate for hours. After all, the Gettysburg Address only lasted for two minutes."

Joan gave me a little shove toward the stage, and once more the crowd magically parted. I walked the ten feet to the steps, climbed up, and made my way to the microphone. The crowd that had seemed huge when I'd walked through it now appeared to go on for miles before me.

I'm not one of those people who fear public speaking more than death, but I prefer to have some idea of what I'm going to say. I took a breath. Breathing seemed like a promising start.

"Um, hello everyone," I said, leaning into the microphone. My voice billowed out, startling me, which got a laugh. I pulled back a little.

"I'd like to thank all of you for coming to our auction tonight," I went on. Maybe that would be enough. But no, the faces before me were expectant. "I—I've just been reminded that the Gettysburg Address was only two minutes long, and I'm going to try to beat Lincoln." Some appreciative chuckles. "You've been so generous with your bidding, I know we've raised a lot of money. Every penny will be used to make improvements to the dog park."

I paused, seeing the dog park regulars in my mind's eye—the dogs romping, the people watching and laughing at their antics. Mrs. Johnson picking up a leaf. "I know some people think a dog park is a crazy idea, but if you have a dog you know how hard it can be for them to get enough exercise. Our dogs can't run loose like they did when we were kids, it's just not safe. So this park is a place where a dog gets to be a dog. It's also the place where I've made some wonderful friends. Some of them have two legs, and some have four, and I—I love them all."

From the corner of my eye I saw Dan, at the side of the stage, give a thumbs up.

"I wouldn't be here tonight if it weren't for my dogs. I know yours are just as wonderful. So if you haven't brought your dog to the park yet, I hope you'll come soon. It's a great place, and because of your generous bids tonight it's going to be even better. Thanks. Thanks for coming."

I gave a little nod, and turned to leave. A wave of applause carried me off the stage. I had to blink away tears to make it safely down the steps to the ground. Kay was waiting and grabbed me for a hug, than Dan hugged us both. We were surrounded by smiling faces. I felt a surge of affection for my town.

Behind me, the auctioneer said, "All righty then. Let's get this road on the show. We have one more lot to sell. You've been waiting to see it, now here's your chance to own a piece of history."

214

I turned back to the stage. The auctioneer held up an object covered with a red silk scarf. His banter continued, the cadence like a barker at a fair.

"You've read the story in the paper, heard it on the radio. You've seen it on TV. Desperate thieves lost a priceless treasure and tried to ransom it back with a kidnapping. So the Duke of Tintesford, who came to Willow Falls to retrieve that ancient piece of art, fooled the thieves by making this replica—" He whipped off the scarf, revealing the lumpy contours of the fake Egyptian frog— "with his very own hands. The golden frog of Ramses the Fourth has been returned to Egypt, but the replica that saved the day is right here, and it can be yours."

I looked at Kay. "Ramses the Fourth?"

She shrugged. "At least he didn't say King Tut."

"Let's start the bidding. Who'll give me fifty?" the chant began.

I was about to exclaim, "Fifty! Who'd pay fifty bucks for a lump of plastic clay?" when a woman standing near me shot up her hand.

"I have the fifty. Seventy five?"

They were off. People scattered throughout the crowd were bidding. The price spiraled up. I couldn't wait to tell Hank about this. I wished he were here to see it.

"We have four hundred seventy five. Who's got five hundred?"

Someone in the back did. The bidding went on. Bidders dropped out as the price rose, but it kept rising. At nine hundred dollars, Kay shook her head and began to laugh. The price went up, advanced now by tens instead of fifties. When it reached nine eighty, Dan gave a little hop of excitement.

On stage, the auctioneer wiped his brow with the red scarf. "We have nine hundred eighty dollars, ladies and gentlemen. We have nine ninety. All right, let's do it. Who's got the thousand?" He paused and scanned the crowd. "Do we have a thousand."

The crowd seemed to hold its collective breath. No one spoke, no hand waved to signal a bid.

"I'm looking for a thousand," he said again, and waited. Silence in the tent. "You'll never have an opportunity like this again, ladies and gentlemen. Do we have the thousand? We have nine ninety...going once—"

A clear contralto voice called out, "One thousand twenty seven dollars!"

The auctioneer beamed. "One thousand twenty seven dollars! Going once! Going twice! Sold to Mrs. Johnson for one thousand twenty seven dollars. Come on up here and claim your prize."

The crowd parted and Mrs. Johnson, with Prince Henri in her arms, made her way to the front. "Close your mouth," Kay hissed in my ear.

Mrs. Johnson gave me a little smile as she mounted the steps, her back as ramrod straight as ever. She walked calmly to the auctioneer and took the vaguely froglike lump from his hand, giving him a regal nod as she did so. Dan began to clap enthusiastically, and the entire tentful of people joined in. Prince Henri stretched out his head to sniff the fake Egyptian frog, then gave it a little lick. People cheered and shrill whistles rang out.

Mrs. Johnson might have been a movie star, accustomed to the acclaim of thousands. She smiled out at the crowd, and just as the applause was beginning to wane, leaned toward the microphone. In a heartbeat, everyone was still.

"Gad, she ought to run for president," Kay mumbled. Mrs. Johnson flicked a glance our way and raised an eyebrow. Then she spoke into the microphone.

"Thank you. Thank you so much. I will treasure this memento, as I've come to treasure this dog park and the kind people who come here. I am new to dog ownership, and I do not know what I would have done without this place. And as some of you know, we have another frog in our living room as well. This will look lovely next to it on my mantel."

The End

About the author:

Sharon Henegar started life in the Midwest, and although she is not in the Witness Protection Program she has lived in 27 houses in seven states. She now resides in a Midcentury Modern home in Salem, Oregon with her storyteller husband, Steven; Edward and Zoë, the Springer spaniel-mix dogs; and cats Noll Baxter and Mrs. Wilberforce. Together they conduct retreats and workshops for writers and storytellers.

Henegar believes in home cooking, the restorative powers of humor and dogs, in buying secondhand, that a convertible should be driven with the top down, that life needs dessert, and that M&Ms should be bought in bulk. She is currently working on the next book in the Willow Falls series.

The Willow Falls Series:

We hope you've enjoyed the third volume of the Willow Falls series. Here's what readers have said about the first two books:

"Light a fire, pour a cup of tea, and enjoy an evening with ... this engaging cozy mystery from Sharon Henegar. Louisa's and Bob's adventures—and misadventures—kept me up way past my usual bedtime...How long must I wait for a sequel?" -Andrea Dietze

"...I found myself not wanting to do anything but keep on reading. Her chapter ending cliff hangers, complete with murder and kidnapping, propel you through the book." -Linda Wight

"*Sleeping Dogs Lie* was so enjoyable. I liked the characters immediately and wished I had a friend just like Louisa. ... I consider it a nearly perfect mystery. Her upcoming new novel *In Dogs We Trust* is even better than the first ... the plot twist was breathtaking." - Teresa Raines

"Characters who become your friends...Don't get me wrong - the baddies are suitably bad and the plot is thrilling. But it is the sympathetic and very real main characters (dogs and humans) in this book who have stayed in my mind - in some way they have become part of my mental landscape and I rather expect to meet them one day. I certainly intend to 'meet' them in the next installment!" -M. Alison Heal

"This was a "can't put it down once you start" book. The characters are so funny and very real. I loved the dogs and their antics. I am looking forward to Sharon's next book. When I say you will Laugh Out Loud, I mean it!" -Linda MacKean

Need more copies of any books in the series? Find more information at www.SaturdayBooks.com!

www.ingramcontent.com/pod-product-compliance
Lightning Source LLC
Chambersburg PA
CBHW070451260626
47161CB00004B/1270